Tula Lies

Tula Lies

Maria Haydee Torres

To order additional copies of this book, contact:
Xlibris
844-714-8691
www.Xlibris.com
Orders@Xlibris.com
850803

Please, daddy doesn't beat my mother.

Contents

Note

Please daddy doesn't beat my mother. This Story corresponds to the first edition now with a little update to the topics, actually I am adding in the 2nd edition continues now with Tula, young lady who was born in a suburb of a town farm from San Felipe, it happened in a distant country from Sur Central.

Both editions are based on fiction story, therefore also all names people are fictitious, places, cities, institutions all those are imaginary.

Two edition in same book following the plot in the 2nd edition now "Tula lies".

Dedication

This book is dedicated to all the victims of domestic violence untrusting For all those people who have suffered from domestic violence it's time to wake up It's time to get up the courage and push forward, No more abuse; you need to confront the abuser doesn't matter if they are family uncle, cousin, step-dad, your own dad, remember that any abuse should be not permitted; none of these: verbal, sexual, physical abuse, do not be afraid to report it, keep insisting, over and over again until the law takes care of them.

Introduction

This is the history of Tula that her first child was born early at seven months of pregnancy as a result of the kicks and beatings inflicted by her husband, in consequence, Tula giving a birth with complications an giving her the name PEGGY, since there they begins the violence domestic for Tula husband.

Tula with great ambition to marry the rich man of the town, at the end got in separation from her husband living as Single mother with four children without support to feed them but Tula continue the life con Peggy daughter, in try doing a best life, but end of years Tula, loses her good feeling and becomes Rude and unfair to her children and relatives, in the end she as an ungrateful mother, many of the topics show how Tula lies.

Chapter # 1

ESTEBAN AND TULA, IN MARRIAGE

Esteban and Tula,, they knew each other since they were kids, were born in the same Tula, make a short description of daily life in his town. the adults are friends, neighbors in community helping each other; children and youth continue the rhythm of life, grow up, some going to school, other fall in love and often get marry to young may be sixteen year old.

but let me tell you that for some youth finding stumbles coming from family, based on gathers and taking everything they want because they have money, silver, land, cattle, properties, would be converted in rich landowners, ranchers farmers based on how much is how powerful they get. The untouchable in the town, where those had power until they just imagine that the law was made for them.

the untouchables, they bought the priests with gifts as gratitude but it was more like a such as a vehicle, money, on Sunday palms of cheese, curd and beans all those for the parish priest, and as always the untouchable rich, every Sunday with their families in the first rows of the Church, very well dressed, so clean with appearance impeccable, untouchable, with the distance very marked the priest always very kind to them the rich of the town were always very talkative and smiling Well look the priest friendly with rich people, by the time the bribes would catch up to them

While with the poor these priests they became grumpy, trying to educate the poor to give a better contribution. But the priest taking and educate to have love for the community but for him, the rich know about civility and love for others, for the priest the rich have the real love for others. I saw the priest with face dog for the poor and the friendly face for the rich people from the town.

The guards of the town, they became the neglected when it came to apprehending one of the rich adults and/or youth man, including their employees and relatives.

For these rich people too had their means of entertainment, music, exotic races horse, like means of entertainment for these, sons, daughters, riding, showing off their best horses.

In this town the routine becomes custom and distractions and traditions exists to make life nice,the best distraction there was a little bar very classic, the owner my grandma Martha, was respected because of her three sibling men who were military, one of them was commander in chief, named Fernando, the captain Leonidas, upon returning from visiting his family and almost already reaching the military base where was located his battalion, they were unaware killing them instantly, believing that they were enemies, they were ambushed This happened in the mountains of the North, it was commented by my grandmother with great sadness when received the news.

Of the three grandmother sibling that Martha the only one left alive was the doctor named Manuel; my grandmother tells me that she was loved a lot because she was the only one sister. He was the first Doctor of the County City respected was loved by the people who knew him.

My grandmother's delight was to comment about his Doctor sibling, she mentioned what His brother after a long week of work they would travel on Saturdays to the farm with the family since they had fun on the farm riding; they cooked their roasts and have a very pleasant time, returning to the County City by early on Mondays.

In that County City, Most of the population is dedicated to

cattle rising and also to agriculture, my grandmother Martha commentedwhat brother liked raising cattle and horses a lot, and he loved riding along with his wife on the farm. This comment, my grandmother always made with a lot of enthusiasm which seemed like she was living in the moment when talking about his family. Now I understand that despite being the owner of a bar my grandma Martha was respected by all the rich of the town, it was because his good siblings, were respected by the wealthy of the town.

Tula made comments about happen in San Felipe town, there was sadness marked her young poor life; there were cases of family girls very poor that appeared pregnant, in some case mothers and daughters, Worst of all from the same man. Sometimes it was not known until many years later,

In the town San Felipe, the only bar visited by the wealthy, was exclusive to the Wealthy people always around to drink their wine to get out of the routine.

My mother Lila procreate three siblings girls: Alexandrina, Esperanza and me Tula. We lived in my grandmother Martha, house, therefore my mother and me helped to my grandmother by working the bar and my sisters Esperanza, Alexandrina, well we lived in the moment without any prejudice as all young girls discovering our environment, most of the times we were around town, gossiping, as all teenager who smile or laughs humorously. When we are in the bar yes looking from a place where we were no visible observing those old men green tail.

The important thing is that my grandmother Martha, no idea that we were flirting

Everyday around four at clock, especially at the same time Esteban appeared, with the excuse of a drink, but I think he had something other than a drink in mind.

As far as I was concerned, in concerning me Tula, my life turning monotonous without imagining that our lives interaction from a social point; where the interactions as humans we make a difference in as for our social core. But up to this point I did not care to know how the social class works.

Well, the word social nucleus did not cross my brain, I've never heard in my home comments about it, therefore there was no reason to worry about my family living situation as I thought they were happy in their own way; really wouldn't like to experience neither think in that of the social nucleus, simply like seeing everything as a friendship that make feel good until now. Many people had heard saying don't cross the line, Ha, Ha, funny word, I just see it like that. I think it's another way of living in our same planet. People crazy What matters to me is what I see and how I feel, really feel happy in my way of living, for the rest I don't care since until now I don't know how it works not to cross the line neither social core .

My sisters girls are without prejudice just like me, although I am the most extroverted, we never put very much attention to the rich of the town, which would constantly arrive at the bar I wondered if they would coming to dink or to see us, the wealthy people of the town we are considered old married green tails. Yea ja, ja its fanny.

But here came two young people to the bar frequent: Esteban and Tony, am beginning to notice frequent visits of these two young men they left before their parents arrived at the bar.

Well we knew us since we were children, but they weren't neighbor, well they would be ignore me; Esteban, is the son of one of the landowners and ranchers one of many rich people front this town. Well now but why the continuous visits from those young people to the bar?

I am very interested in Esteban! Every time; they arrive over and over, I am feeling very anxious. They came daily; upon his arrival look like so funny, and elegantly they asked for one a drink, talking friendly they would stay for an hour, and then left.

Days and months passing, I started to make a plan; the grandma house is big and we would look for an appropriate place for when they arrived I could observe, I found a very suitable one where we could see each other, but making sure my Grandmother would not see us; I never gave him a clue or hint that I was interested in the most known young man of the town where all the girls knew of him

It would be Great if my grandma would ever considered me her personal bodyguard, because every time they appeared in the bar, I would sit down as a little good girl, they also watched me well from time to time and when Esteban secretly look at me; hmm I would think he just had sympathy for me .

The days and months were passing, but nothing changed I

always expected that something between Esteban and me would be happen, in the same place in the house, at the same time in expectation of the unimaginable.

Here comes the most beautiful thing, several months have passed, his frequent visits provoked me to get closer little by little with them, secretly the best way is going with my grandmother, with the excuse just asking _for my mother lily, who was supposedly she is not there in the kitchen?; It was my first day to get their attention, It was true I, felt a little embarrassed that neither I realized what I had caught his attention.

At this time me Tula, was already feeling a special attraction something in my heart that made it beat by Esteban. I no wait more me provoked to get closer to them to the point that every time they arrived; I tried to be around them and located a place where he could also observe me.

At to this time wonder this will be colling flirting or to be in love good. One drop of water daily to a bucket reaches the point where it overflows and this is the way; I felt the infatuation for Esteban, and without a doubt I was convinced that he arrived only to see me. He did not hide his interest for me.

Up to this point I had not thought about the relationship seriously, just a flirt, but it is me liking him.

Well at my age, and living in a town in the type of community where we are friends, what obstacle could happen Yeah could be my boyfriend or his girlfriend, but I had no doubt and was not thinking about it. I am very young and also him, may be falling in love and thinking no one would interfere in our lives.

Now I was feeling that our infatuation compared to a bottle where the air in and out only could only be stop with a plug. So I always saw my life of youth like the bottle without a stopper. Now I will give expansion to my feelings and everything was like lightning, a Unlimited attraction; that sounds good .Until now nothing that breaks the fire nor the sparks fly.

I wonder how far this attraction would go. With Esteban, did not hide always he was over like he was the bar owner; and my grandmother house look like his house it's going nice.

The attraction turned stronger, a crazy love without measure no cons familiar Consequence; the other side of the coin was my family As if nothing was going here, no comment or suggestion; everything fine as the water flows in the river.

Up to this point I could not distinguish the difference my family looked our engagement as part of daily life without prejudice nor obstacles, therefore everything smelled like marriage.

Never at home I listened to comments about the poor or the rich, I thought we were equal living our own emotions as all majority of young people mindless dreamers, in the future just living in the moment and how beautiful when a feeling of attraction exists.

Well the months were passing by, and the attraction grew more an more, no comment on it, his family did not interest me at the moment and what I was feeling was unstoppable love for him . I don't know what I would do If one day stopped seeing him.

But here the unexpected comes; His no appear, one day, two days, three days, was gone. I was worried, what could have happened, what happened to him?

Wondered if he was going to be alone and thought would be with other girl. Will be in love with another girl?. What's wrong with him? if Will be sick? I don't know but I won't look for him either because if I realize that he is with another girl, I don't know what would do? Neither imagine for today should be stop in thinking in him, could be have good news tomorrow.

Today three days have pasted, and no news of Esteban, he has not visited it made me disturbed, but I'm sure that something is wrong, but Here comes the doubt, could it be that he got tired of me or maybe the passion has passed?; well I won't know any way Be patient and I'll see what happens in the next days. Already they haven't come to visit for four days, for now! I will hope to have a surprise

Next day already four days, very worried waiting for the day to pass quick to see if I would have news on Esteban, yeah almost ten in the morning, for a moment my eyes remain fixed looking in front of the door; over there I see people entering the bar, Just like nothing has happened there he is without any excuse very friendly and sneakily approached discreetly and told me in secret, saying can I discuss in private something very important with you? that fine responding Tula, seeing Esteban I will wait in the square in front of the church, Tula, confirm made a gesture with my frowning face the same one that has brought this man in his mind?

After the message, he turned around and as usual did joke with my grandmother calling her old lady, how is it going in your bar? And without waiting for an answer he responds quickly just to saying I have to go back I'm doing a little job with my dad, giving her a pat on the hand.

Me Tula, I am at the point of curiosity to know what the secret he will tell me in private. I can't deny that I am already in love of Him, now the idea of losing him worries me, I wonder if it will be that Esteban feels he same feeling of which I feel for him? the doubt really bothers me since I have fallen in love so much that I want to be his wife, what nonsense what I am saying, but look good my idea but really I don't know his intentions, coming back to reality I tell myself Tula no more dream.

Nonsense nothing more, I am thinking as a little girl daydreams, its nice but it really is dreaming; need to wake up, I can't deny attracts me a lot, he's handsome, now also his money could be a better life for me. By myself What happens Tula?; what happen It's not love, but not price for dream it will be many time, sometime a dream will be coming thru, that fine, anymore I think I 'm confused? That fine, everything is to be seen.

I feel very excited, uh, it will be that the secret could telling me that he loves me and saying do you want to marry me! The idea not leaves sleep and I wonder smiling and moving mischievously my eyes doing other things, moving my head to the side to other. Now wonder why I have never noticed him before.

After meditating my future without losing time I direct myself to the place that Esteban told me, this is the time to know what He want tell me, of something that I am not sure of, will this help plan my next expectation to secure our courtship, well, there is nothing else to think about, you have to get out doubt, without saying anything I left my home and get heading to the address he has given me.

how far can I go being I am a person in love and curious, still walking fast to get the place indicated; walked so fast that make me felt like a dog with my tongue sticking out, because the town has streets with a lot of steep hills and down hills, and we living in the lower part of the town and Esteban, in the higher part of town two blocks from the Church.

Walking quickly, until finally almost arriving, my curiosity was indescribable; in the distance could be appreciate that He is there waiting for me, I approaching and Esteban, also came to meet me half way and we were face to face, with love he took me in his arms and we walked to the address, at I thought that he was looking for a place to sit down, and be able to discuss comfortably. We arrived at the porch of the Town Court and there we sat down

When we were both sitting comfortably, I asked him; well here tell me what you wanted to say in private? He just looked me on my face and said I want us to get married today. I looked at him shocked looking into his eyes I couldn't digest what he had just told me, thought it was a joke; I asked how are we supposed to get married? we will marry in the court with the judge Ramón,. I asked who else would be there. He answered, well my best friend, the Judge You and Me, and no one else.

I questioned Esteban, what will happen to my family? He said everything will be good but we won't tell them yet. I will not return home, that's right, and the opposite is not getting married and each one will go their separate ways it's like this, or not get marriage, for today you will not return to your house, tomorrow we will tell them that we have married and I'm I 'm sure they won't say anything, you family will be happy.

I stayed quiet for some minutes ; up to that point nothing on my mind Not even thinking that it was Esteban's plan, I just thought was all this a product of the love that he had for me, I pursed my lips nodding down toward as affirming the fact of getting married, and I said to myself I already did it, so it seemed that I had won the jackpot i thought The idea of " getting married " was fantastic, I didn't care if the dress the veil on my head, none of that mattered to me .

I wondered would you agree. I replied yes with up and down head movement gesture confirming that I accepted; Esteban, without thinking about neither say nothing took two steps forward and raising his arm and pointing with the palm of the outstretched hand said Lets go to court. very slowly I moved forward, I do not deny that at that moment I felt nervous and shy I saw the judge, and greeted him we sat very quietly in front of the judge and brainstorm floating in my brain, only ideas that coming to my main, asking by myself really He is love me?.

Pursed my lips and made a gesture saying okay, I'll get married.

there the Judge Ramón at his desk it would seem that he already knew Esteban's plan, no doubt it was planned; now I just didn't understand why he disappeared for four days, at the moment the civil marriage proceeded, and everything was done so quickly and without losing time such it seemed that the Judge and Esteban were afraid of something; Esteban and me Standing also the witness who is the best friend the name Tony.

The judge asked if we were ready answering quickly Esteban, say yes Sir, immediately looked at the clock, exactly four in the afternoon, time where we were in ceremony position; it was so fast, we stood up, said the oath phrases together until the eternity, signing and married; everything was done very fast so that I did not notice to see the time when it finished but it was so fast I calculated some twenty minutes .

At the end of the ceremony, humorously the friend asked where wills the honeymoon be? he said mocking ; I really ignored, we are now husband and wife, the honeymoon was not really in my plans, But Tony still with fanny joked and smiled at me. At the point I felt very upset I had to say him that enough stop you stooped joke it's no fanny.

The Judge seemed somewhat restless; you could tell his expression of concern no comment, the Judge uncle Esteban's not imagine the claims from the Esteban Parents, for to had married to his favorite son.

just ridiculous ideas, nonsense of old ways we are legal age; Esteban has twenty three years old and me eighteen, what we are doing, why think in what we do not know, of what they will say the parents of who is today my husband .

Already in my moments of worry, I do not deny in feel bad daughter, the feeling of conscience begins to disturb me for not having told Mama that I would meet with Esteban and now I'm married with Him, but my arrogance was so strong that the feeling for my mother remained there.

Well the truth is that I don't even have the idea, now reality I have married him young further handsome and rich from the town, good the life gives us surprises beautiful and this is one for me, making a gesture pursing my lips affirmative, as saying I already did it..

After the civil marriage, we say goodbye to the Judge, and Esteban friend; we hold hands and we headed to the Esteban house, they lived very near the Court about _ three blocks away, we walk very excited very sticky as all couples in love and newly married; well I'll see what comes by honeymoon and it's really gone _ on my list enjoy a _ honeymoon is the _ _ desire of everything newly married, however I think that honeymoon is to be together loving each other, well no more imagination, I squeezed his hand and we both walked shut up

I really did not imagine the thoughts of me now husband mine, well it was two blocks but I felt them so far just thinking he welcome from my now parents in-laws, finally we arrived and I began to feel Little scared, nervous maybe because I really didn't know which It would be the reaction of Esteban's parents .

We entered the house and Esteban suggested that sit down in the living room while going with my parents, taking long strides with a small little cough as clearing his throat trying to get attention; but it didn't take long a lot in their parents appear with a face not very friendly .

Esteban's parents suspected that something queer was passing; when seeing me with his son ; now my husband, showed a character unusual was noticeable very happy and funny with his parents, the greeting and without losing time told them ; I present to you my wife Tula, now you know her about _ all You Father. Without hesitation he told them what some minutes we have contracted civil marriage.

the unexpected news I leave the parents almost inert with courage, Celia, Esteban's mother, with the eyes very open and his father Mr. Francisco, as always with his respectful features, well dressed in ironed pants and sleeved shirt long light blue color, her countenance was _ pale, really I can't even imagine what they were thinking well they knew my family especially Mr. Francisco, since he was one of those who went to my grandma Martha's bar.

Mr. Francisco, in fact, was not pleasing the news; they looked like as bugs weird, I could appreciate that they were not accepting as we expected, I do not deny that I felt very uncomfortable ashamed and my only fault is falling in love with Esteban, the vibe feels _ very intense nobody comment about it; my now husband fixed my gaze about their parents without any comment, he took me by the hand and led me to his room.

Already in the room could give I fly to my feelings feeling me as a despicable rat, it was not my fault that they did not accept me like his wife son, that joy that I felt when I got married had vanished he same day of our marriage, staying broken my heart; sadness intoxicated me, there could give me account of the differences social and felt the contempt for being poor, what else could think it was just a poor and they did not like the news of our marriage .

I leave fall on the bed in fetal position, actually felt die to the point that I fell asleep crying without consolation..

I was wondering one and other time, being poor is a crime? Really when I got married it was very innocent as all young girl not Knows neither measure the differences and think that everything in life is love,

But not; there are always setbacks very strong that eats away the feelings of soul.

Today I understand the words saying do not crossing the line, the famous social core. Today I can feel sadness; my happiness is framed in those sad phrases, because before those phrases did not work for me, because my mother and grandmother never explain, well two things they never thought that Esteban would marry me, the other is that a marriage could work with me, I was a bad girl, I was filled with ambition really this is my consequence now .

I think I crossed the line, and when I crossed I lost my naivety, my innocence, because for me there was no social differences, I felt happy together with my family, now I am unhappy I have crossed the line and I have burned myself .

I wonder which was it my sin in reality _ it was a sin make my dream reality by marrying with the man of my dreams

But I didn't go that far until the day I married Esteban, I could give me realize that it was not easy get along, a poor man with a rich man ; because Now I've realized that really the obstacles they exist, it is a very big and hard to understand . to my early age just thought in love my way and nothing else .

Now who can yes me had blame for my misfortune? Why not guide me to the differences of social class? The only thing I can say is that there is no law in the heart that you help to discern for the person to fall in love with. I wonder will it be that the heart of the rich works with a special feeling that tells them when and where chooses his partner. Could it be that the Rich are happy?, in my way of living I did not look obstacles I thought they didn't exist differences, and that love was free to which it came.

Now I think that Esteban, my mother and grandmother left me play coin _ face or sun I'm sure that they knew about the social nucleus and its differences.

However in the morning next I woke up and sat up in he bed edge; _ and another time I started to feel guilty feeling _ since I had ran away from my mother's house and thought in the concern that it would be causing for my disappearance _

Yet I felt my stomach empty hunger grunt _ since we had not Eaten for about seventeen hours, trying to put in order our marriage bond to the point that we both lost he appetite to eat

in regards _ to Esteban, you could tell very relaxed looking at the roof of the house, nor thought in go get something to eat for both of us simply suggested that I do it since there are early hours no one in the kitchen and since he did not know the house, what he did was tell me as get to and prepare something to eat for both of us, what I could think, is that Esteban, feared meet her _ mother in the kitchen, no way I didn't have option and I went to prepare some breakfast .

It was approximately six in the morning, Esteban, he told me that nobody It would in the kitchen and in fact when we got to the kitchen there was no one, I started looking a dish pan to prepare a breakfast fast such as do some eggs; when suddenly _ I feel a sensation as Yeah someone watching me spontaneously turn my head and there Celia my mother-in-law, a young woman of some forty years old, with skin color pale and appearance elegant, she looked at me very fit, hard to understand his feelings such she followed standing there and little by little her face was taking a anger posture that something brought against me, for a moment she began to release his language telling me many depreciably words hard for me to understanding; She still telling me If you think that by marrying Esteban, your life will be going to change for something better in you economic lifer?, you were wrong, nor in dream, you will be continue throwing tortilla like you did in your house, now pay attention ; look in that place on the right side of the kitchen over there is a sack of corn, in the next left door over there is the stone to grind corn, don't expend the time making now tortilla, which is the only thing you know how to do submissively without saying any words just listen and started do everything that She, indicated the task of making tortillas, when was looking for the grinding stone and the corn, I tried for not crying, but I couldn't holding back tears, felt humiliated wished go out in a hurry as bitch scared _ The comparison is ugly and not pleasant but it is in reality what is me happening, it's unheard of .

Now I am the Esteban's wife, and I don't know as step back from my situation being young very confuse, but the ambition broke my peace of my diary live.

I felt my dreams and love vanished, to the point that my ambition frame my life in sadness, I wanted give up everything _ There, I realized that being poor _ has much courage and dignity, and I had to face my misfortune ambitious and I could appreciate that it is better to be poor with dignity because before I got married I was happy _ And really happiness does not have price was happy to my way of living simple, innocent and wanting to live as all young in love

The days of marriage without honeymoon, I am living the opposite of one true honeymoon.

Day by day pass in marriage, but the atmosphere of disgust remained the same, the rejection of Esteban's family, for me it is so evident.

My parents in law constantly they held their meetings with my husband careful that I could not listen the conversation.

They held their meetings; I think to see the way to separate us.

I still working in the in the kitchen there was no difference between the employee and me, there the two of us in the kitchen doing the tortillas, were day by day until in one those day in early morning Mr. Francisco, calling privately to my husband, instantly I thought they were up to something could be a plan to separate us? Now it's only my turn wait to know what they are talking with my husband. Worried to know what was happening, he told me also, something must be going already they have almost an hour in meeting, curiosity worries me.

At the end of the meeting with his parents, I saw Esteban coming, in kitchen address.

I told myself I think I'm not wrong about my concerns about their parents, I shouldn't get ahead of the events I'll see what happens Esteban arrive to the kitchen telling me follow me, let's go to the room we have to talk; without comment I followed him, now in he on the way to the room he told me the wishes of his father; in fact tea I say take the news lightly positive thinking as any newly married Seeing the prospects of establishing a home . Very good Esteban yes everything is for keep our marriage it would be fine for me, the only thing that worries me is to be living here at your parents' house, I sit uncomfortable and humiliated, I prefer return to my mother

Tula exactly that is what we will talk about; since my parents are thinking that we should move. I will say their plan. _ I don't know how will you take it but today my father has suggested that we must move to one of their farms dedicated to growing and raising cattle, this farm is not very far from town and now he suggest I need fend for myself I need work for my matrimony, since I am now a married man and the best way is to work for us themselves, well I answered ; it seems to me Your idea of moving from your house is very good . Really your parents have reason is the best we should do.

I see a good outlook for future plans together.

In the end, I answered to my husband but don't worry I will go where you decide. In this house I feel ashamed a thief without a cause, I feel humiliated and you know._

my husband left the room, but I don't stay there all my imagination begins to solidify the idea of moving but to some extent the news makes me feel happy, upon hearing Mr. Francisco's proposal to move from his house, this seemed to me fantastic, my in-laws doing the right, because we need working for own matrimony. Rather our relationship bond will be solidified. Fine is time in preparer to the move.

Chapter # 2

ESTEBAN AND TULA, COURSE TO THE TEMPORARY HOME

Well the change it was so fast that the next day we were coming out toward our new temporary home, if you could say home.

Well it came the day and us we went to the farm, really a bit sad, we don't had nothing at all, we didn't have the little clothes he brought set some many necessary by my husband, since he did not allow me return home, for to get my clothes.

We arrived at the farm, it was sad and desolate, we tried to get a little comfortable, well the panorama was not welcoming, it did not have conditions to say that it was worth he change ; that yes _ any stuff I would be better than being living at my in-laws house .

The only thing that cheered me up in continue ahead is the hope of improving, it is possible say it that the field made me feel melancholic. not electing could notice to Esteban, a little worried without making no comment, what it did to me feel a little bad since I was thinking that he did not trust in me, in telling his problems or future plans .

However, I understand Esteban's frustration, because his routine life has changed _ completely, it will no longer be treaty as he son capricious, and that situation maybe it is what is mortifying, well no more I,Guess it will pass.

But at that moment not only him this concerned

also, it has already happened a week and I have not tried to contact my mother and tell her that I have married Esteban, I think that he is really not well, it strange is that I have not heard no comment about my disappearance by part of my mother

Could it be that they don't care? Maybe they

Suspect that I 'm leaving with Esteban, the sign for my mother and grandmother is that he has not returned to the bar. And they must think that it is the best that he could for me happen when I run away with Him.

Tula, Tula, always conjecture, it really is the truth to this time has passed more than one week and no comment and if would have. Another day, already _ relaxed in my bed I can't stop thinking about the contempt that I have lived by part of my husband's parents when I got married.

If my mother knew about the slights humiliating that they made me from Esteban's family, I think that I would have already come to get out of this house, well in the same way they must know of my absence, tonight I will write a letter informing you of the marriage I contracted, I hope that Matilde delivers my little note to my mother, and I think that receiving it will make her feel good.

As the days go by I feel a little more relaxed all the same could observe that my husband was taking their work days seriously, with the I take care of the cattle, and the communication with the butler or foreman as usually tell those who work _ care of the farm etc. On the third day the unexpected comes for me when he tells me that in the morning he would go to town since he needed talking with his father about some vaccines and food for cows..

Chapter # 3

COMPLICATED MARRIAGE

well what else say I have to start in rely in Esteban, but here already comes the problem almost day by day, the excuses were you could continue say every days his get trips to town with the justification of buying products for the farm, their outputs you continue to bother me but did not have option, was spending a month, two months of married, then I notice that my menstrual period has stopped, _ discomfort stomach as vomiting was continuous, it does not fit doubt they are the first pregnancy symptoms I am _ experiencing.

notwithstanding though the symptoms made me feel sick at the same time felt a sensation pretty with just him fact we'll have a child, also got excited just thinking in break the news to my husband and I hope that he also excited to know that He will be "DAD". but He have a problem his departures continue and constant and arrivals late home and smelling of alcohol, this situation is me worrying and worst of all, I had no one by my side to talk and appease my worries, he did not allow me visit my family, and every day the news of my pregnancy dragged on has not given me the opportunity to give him the beautiful news because every time he returns now comes drunk every day is done difficult because Esteban has not been in talking conditions.

"WANTED GIVING THE GOOD NEWS, BUT IT WAS DESAPEAR LITTLE BY LITLE, UNTIL IT HAS VANISHED THE EMOTION TO HAVE A BABY.

We're going the days and without giving him the news, the months go by and my stomach growing up and Esteban, ignoring me without noticing anything about my pregnancy, because the drunkenness of liquor makes it impossible for him and the news of giving him about my pregnancy vanishes _ each time what try to say the good news.

His behavior was Changing it was no longer him drunk quiet that he came and sat down in the room until falling asleep; now begin by ask me for food that is not really within my reach beef soup, impossible since the meat and the vegetables we can only obtain all the Saturdays, when the butler does the market of the week

the most difficult when at midnight he ask me for his cravings and many sometimes I don't have what he You want to eat, and the worst thing is that get angry, I can understanding is a simple excuse to start a discussion .

I am worrying has become aggressive like a madman without control, throwing blows for all sides, just to start in fight toward me, I don't know what can do; he looks like a lion attacking its prey .

what can I do saying Tula run away to my grandmother's house, He began to hit me, doing it as a habit ; today He is hitting very ugly, I will lose my pregnancy, until I can't stand it more and I yelled at him, don't hit me, I am pregnant. Regardless of my pregnancy; the liquor made him lose control of their actions.

up to here the pretty ones arrived illusions of breaking the news to my husband about my pregnancy, I only remain in thought, now only worry thinking how far really they will arrive the mistreatment .

The day after the beating I woke up sore, getting dressed made me difficult had a lot of pain and bruises by all sides of the body. He went crazy with alcohol, now I have fear of escaping and that he would come looking for me and the situation would turn further difficult. What can I do? Stay here, it's my consequence. I am paying my fault.

Chapter # 4

TULA SADNESS

He baby in my belly I feel that it is developing quickly; to this time already I have seven months the good thing is that in about two more months I will give birth like this as actually I am seing the months go by fast.

Today I got up with bad presentiment that overwhelms me something bad It will happen with my pregnancy, something anguishes me. good already The day is almost over and everything is fine, the next day is also fine, like this were going the days, arrive Saturday of a lot worry since Esteban, lately appears drunk and the fight It starts, after the fight, He leaves home like nothing happens.

Now they have Four days have passed and he doesn't show up, well, if it's for discussions with blows, it's better if he doesn't even show up, I don't feel well.

I will take a good rest that will help me to meditate, now resting in bed, I started with a feeling of reproach saying, now nothing is staying of him good feeling that I have felt for Esteban, it is disappearing, now I don't know, for their acts He is the only one to blame for my sadness, your little game by falling in love was made hell for me, in his head full of caprice and now that He has broken my life, my feelings, my innocence and love also for live, I have sad, in my heart. Only live now for my new coming baby coming soon.

Today is Friday, no way to wait for it's almost twelve noon; I started to feel hungry is time to make some food I going to the kitchen to prepare myself something to eat; When I finished cook, I served my plate of food late it went to the dining room to take my lunch, when done, I was left without the desire to do anything, my stomach felt so full and to digest better my lunch I started to clean the _kitchen, then I went to the room to have a little nap for true._ I stayed asleep approximately twenty minutes, when suddenly I woke up hearing a loud noise; a little scared stayed sit on the edge of the bed putting up attention in waiting for more noise, stayed sitting in bed, _thinking _ in the noise that was listened already I was almost on my feet when suddenly I could seeing Esteban in front of me, it was almost three in the afternoon, you could tell disoriented, drunk and hostile demanding food like always_ .

I when mentally prepared by myself, saying the same thing another fight other time demanding food, the worst does He not like my food there for I preparer food something for me since He only appears on Saturdays, bad luck today for my misfortune it is to cry with sadness, now neither tears come out by my eyes for so much that I had cried .

really felt sick, I started to feel pain in my stomach, will be nerves? I replied I will prepare something. Asking me for food it is only excuse, well, he did not hesitate in tell me you don't have food. The food t was a excuse enough reason to attack me with kicks and punches Itried to defend myself but Impossible I couldn't with his aggressiveness and without anyone to defend me .That day I couldn't more, I could no longer defend myself, I felt die.

Chapter # 5

FORCE * BIRTH* CAUSE
BEATINGS from a DRUNKEN husband.

It seems that it satisfied to him see me roll in he I floor, and Him, cowardly leave as if there was nothing past at home; while I remained dying of pain,

After this beating, hours more _ late I started to feel pains treble and contractions, such as consequence of the beatings as I was able to get up and go laid on bed, I felt an agonizing pain, my regrets They were so strong that they arrived at the house of Efrain, the foreman of the farm, and his wife Tomasita, went straight to my room she came up to my bed as soon as I saw her look countenance and was very concern, telling her; help me please, am dying, She told me I will go by Ephraim, and went out quickly from the room, and was in looking for Efrain, comments Tomasita saying She need a Doctor; the situation is not in my hands.

Tula, is dying, hurry with a broken voice other time repeats the farm boss it is dying, there was no finished explaining _ when my husband told me follow me and we heading quickly to the house patterns .

Quickly we entered the house and the first scene that I saw was Esteban, thrown in a chair completely drunk snored like a demon; without losing time I went with Tomasita to the boss's room, enough see her and I told my wife you stay here, get a towel and dry sweat you can do something for her, I'll go to town in looking for one midwife.

When I got to Town, the first thing I did was look for one of the best midwives I knew Mrs. Rosa, without hesitation I left luckily straight home over there was, in a few words I explained what was happening to the boss 's. Rosa, without thinking twice, answered me; neither talk in march, and we They went to the farm, when Rosa arrived, entered Quickly, he gave a brief salute and headed for the room.

Without losing time put in practiced her midwifery skills and quickly realized account that the Birth was complicated, putting to the fullest your midwifery knowledge trying to save the life of Tula and the baby near born.

The news spread by all he towns commenting that Tula, Esteban's wife, is dying with him baby in his stomach.

The dramatic news was heard by several people and these They came to Esteban's family . Hearing what was

Happening to his daughter-in-law. They quickly went to the farm very sad; the news from Tula about the complications of childbirth.

When they got home they could see the dramatic scene of his drunken son as usual; _ feeling embarrassed, and without saying a word, Celia went to talk with Tomasita, who was sitting fairly almost at the entrance to the room, where Tula battled with strong pains trying to give birth.

I approached and discreetly asking Tomasita, something happened to her, why does she only have scarce seven months pregnant _ Tomasita was discreet and did not a lot comment about it saying right now doesn't have case talk about it, the matters is that your daughter-in-law and he baby come out of danger, answered Celia, for supposed you be right Topmast, we'll talk after all _ this out of danger, answering Tomasita very politely Very good Mrs. Celia. Surreptitiously gave myself the turn and walk towards the room exactly on the right side over there was in a little room, I settled in privately knelt down and said my prayers to heaven asking GOD to save my daughter-in-law along with her baby .

Comment by herself Tomasita, very upset with Esteban, My employers are not to blame for the acts of the son so I'll be on the lookout in what I could help them

Tomasita waiting for her employers following his movements, appreciating that the another angle of the house is found Stephen 's father the corridor watching fixedly an image of JESUS CHRIST; over there was by some twenty minutes, then he went toward the kitchen; followed him quickly and ask again if I could help? and he answered me Yeah look for a candle; I answered him, I know where there are candles, wait here and back in some moments,exactly expend five minutes and I bring it, I back to the place indicated in a small drawer they kept waivers, I could see over there a small box of candles, I took one and went to deliver the candle to Mr. Francisco, returning quickly to the corridor where the image of the Virgin Mary was located, for true the whole family very devotees of the virgin Over there lit the candle and made his prayer, in his face could be show the sadness and /or conscience he felt .

Esteban's parents prayed to God for a miracle so that Tula and her newly born about lived, since for Esteban's parents would be his first grandson.

At this point Estevan woke up with the bad news of what he was happening to his wife by consequence of the beating that gave him the day before.

Tomasita, continued sitting at the entrance to the door of the Tula room, no comments was problems of the patterns; just observe and collaborate as much as we can serve them

Life is going away,* Tula, battling death and the midwife Rosa, on the verge of despair and almost giving by overdue since it was putting up complicated he childbirth, family ought prepare for the worst since the mother and he baby about to die When suddenly I see entering through the living room to Chela, Tula's aunt, who also there was been midwife by many years in the City of Boaco. Chela, since entered the room said; I have heard the news related to the difficult delivery, and it is not possible that my niece die of childbirth; quickly in to his niece room and started do up to further difficult efforts by save both lives.

But really the situation was not that easy, it was not a delivery that required techniques traditional, and there was no time to remove her from the farm since they would die on the way, Chela in see the situation told the rest of the family; saying Seeing how difficult the birth was, only a miracle from God would keep her and the baby safe. When Chela was coming back to the room, she stopped at the door looking at Tomasita face she said enters you Also to the room to help me, Tomasita no bacillus quickly they entered the room .

in the room all the relatives present they only looked at each other with each other without comments, Tomasita, very restless, he job this being hard for Chela, everyone at home we just wait a good news, Esteban's parents noticed too much worried, such it seemed that the conscience was blaming by the tragedy of Tula.

While Esteban, sitting in a chair in the patio did not dare to show its face to the family, it was obvious embarrassed, what a shame, yes in I really had it and conscience by his savagery.

Tomasita, commenting to by herself same full of much courage without power do nothing about it since their opinions have no _ validity neither argue with them

Since they are the bosses and us simply the employees, at this point just try to cooperate as much as possible to save the life of Tula and he baby.

Chapter # 6

THE BABY GAVE THE BREATH OF LIFE

At the end of so much effort, it was heard a voice of joy saying THE BABY coming, baby came out, is born! Born, Tomasita, hearing that news quickly enter in the room to help, I looked at Chela, who was sweating copiously, She did all the necessary and ran quickly with the baby to an extra bed that trying to get the cry of life baby, such It seemed that I would not live, so much struggle to save his life, when suddenly a scream was heard acute and it was the new baby, Chela said, both safe, my niece was saved and she was born a lovely little girl apparently safe .

Tula, comments saying he effort It was worth it, I feel so happy that neither the pain I feel I'm very excited with my precious baby It will be my great company, with it my sorrows will not remain neither in I remember

Aunt Chela, taking my newborn, looking at with great admiration felt so happy Chela covered well and put on my chest excited to have her with me, with tears in my eyes, giving thanks to the eternal God by our lives saved, I began to see toward he ceiling as wanting see the sky, little by little it was watching a ray of sun coming in through a hole in the ceiling toward the center of my bed almost about me; I stopped looking at him sun reflection without thinking nothing else, I took a look at the right side of the sunbeam behind pass the beam that stops he ceiling, could not to see well the image that is next to the ray of sun, little by little I looked fixed as I could observe a lump strange that it caught my attention since I am seeing a lump not well defined ; I stayed stare to see Very good Image, to my surprise, there was a enormous snake along the beam to the ceiling looking at us intensely on my bed

instantly _ a sensation of terror ran through my body the snake us looked, I tried to control my fear just thinking that the snake I fell about we imagining the worst ; with gestures disguised I called my aunt Chela, she came over and in whispers I told her what was passing, telling her to take the baby very carefully and take care her in to the other room and notifies the people who are in the living room and tell them to do something to lower the snake, I stayed there in a panic, very rigid waiting for the worst without taking my eyes off the snake .

I couldn't move I felt paralyzed with fear just thinking it falling over me.

in the room they had several relatives, children women and men, Chela left the room and addressed those who were in the room, and told them to wait outside and try to have a stick to protect themselves, because in he roof of the house there is a immense snake about TWO METERS LONG, men held sticks to protect themselves while they try catch the snake, trying to throw it to the other side of the wall facing the street.

Chapter # 7

THE MISTERY OF THE SNAKE

While men try to catch the snake, just thinking about the snake that at one point could fall on top of me, without making any further movement, little by little I left sliding out of bed until able leave the room, and walking very slowly I achieved get to the room, there could breathe better when suddenly I hear a loud noise that made me shock he sound was as a heavy full bag of sand falling from a high place to the ground ..

Now I wonder _ how much time the snake was there and how did the snake reach that place? And precisely when was giving birth, I wonder by how much time was over there calmly the viper? To my cries of pain, with so much movement in and out of people helping Tula and the snake did not move. Who could tell me why what the snake does not us attacked nor did he leave the place ?

what attracted to the snake to my room?. the mystery of the sunbeam, coming out of the roof until it reached my bed, if there hadn't been past that ray of sun I would not have seen the viper; questions and more questions without any answers about the snake.?

After a few minutes I left feeling in a state of calm, and that is when you ask Aunt where my baby is there, can you bring it to me please?

I feel the calm in my heart, I am very happy with my precious girl, after many _ emotions, talk to my in-laws if they could see happiness _ also in their faces from having their first little granddaughter and then they left also they needed rest .

until this moment my husband has not done presence ; neither I want to know where is the most sure it should be taking liqueur celebrating the birth of the baby I think I 'll be in peace by a few days. Although I don't know what will happen tomorrow?

Now I'm living moments in peace, no mistreatment, already Tula chose the daughter name calling "PEGGY, saying my precious Peggy.

Chapter # 8

PEGGY SINCE WAS BORN

Since Peggy born, nothing changed, saying Tula, I feel that I am living a miserable life, Esteban, doesn't make the slightest effort by change, the alcoholism is _ leading to live as a wretch, lost he interest by we.

Although, his continued behavior and I criticized him for my delivery I think it's the best opportunity to move to the town "SAN FELIPE" because here is not life for my baby.

I'm fighting with the time; what's my fault? I am sad because she has born of a family where her father is an alcoholic out of control of himself, with a gloomy character due to alcoholism.

I never imagined that by moving to Esteban parents' farm, it has been the most mistake of my life full of torment for cause of my husband with domestic violence.

Why me had to deserve a husband drunk and abuser, irresponsible, without a bit of tenderness for me and his daughter?

Now I just have to have a little optimism and decision; to move from this place sad, since I can't feel not a bit of enthusiasm by live here, now what matters to me is to give my little Peggy, a bit of security.

Well, the critical way in which my daughter gave birth, for not having the media doctors necessary in this place, now is the best excuse to move with my baby to town.

I have enough time to plan the move, the justification already have it now, only have Esteban, and mother in-law accept my transfer to the town. I know it will be a little difficult since my in-laws consider me part of their farm employees.

My in-laws think that I will live here are wrong, just to think that one day Esteban will kill beating me.

Really Yeah I love my daughter, the best thing I have to do is make the determination to escape from this hell, whether my in-laws and my husband don't give me the Permission, I try because it should be as soon as possible.

but I have fear of my husband and forced me to stay here; no way we have to wait, something will occur to me tomorrow .

the days go on happening exhausted, feel an eternity, exhausted, tired of making plans and without any result, I wonder what if try my escape if it doesn't work?, well neither think how will feel, well I will be positive.

There are days that I lose hope, and sadness overwhelms, day more day and ideas float for my mind seeing the way to escape from here, I'm very convinced that in this farm makes me feel melancholic, scared, and many times without the spirit of fighting by continue go ahead, the worst not thing tried in tell my mother and grandmother they are defenseless to the power of Esteban, something good will occur to me.

When further overwhelmed I feel, it is there when I lean in my daughter since just by seeing her I feel that she is the engine of my existence and makes me fight so hard for one better life for her obviously me too.

The days go by, and I don't stop talking to myself, so what's my turn I'm alone, I will find the way out of this exhausting farm. Now Everything bothers me, my in-laws don't care much about the farm less know he hell I am living ; since my baby was born they have past six months and no day have seen them for here is a show they don't care this place.

My husband's drunk he doesn't even care well he alcoholism

won't let him think, and if my in-laws are thinking that I will continue working getting along with the farm problems and pawns or workers, have been wrong, and I won't, although there are times I think in the butler, and his wife Tomasita, They are very honorable I will remember a lot I will come to visit, but can't stay to live in this place; well the butlers are accustomed, and ESTEBAN, he is friendly with them .

Other sunset and after having _ made he daily chore and tired of thinking and thinking _ all the day, I go to the room to prepare the bed to sleep with my baby, after he has fallen asleep, I I also rested on the bed, thinking in my husband, to the point of depression and little by little tears surround my eyes feeling me confused and sad and another once told me if _ same if Esteban were not drunk maybe we would have found in this farm a place by which to live, working together and building a better future for the three; But no, nothing to do now the luck is cast for me _

The dawn of the day I don't want neither get up now I feel that I am losing control, but I don't have option, I have to do the fight by get up soon my baby will have hungry; I need get up, there is that sadness I have, I am overwhelmed to where I will arrive, because I cannot make the decision to escape, I 'm terrified of Esteban.

sunsets worry me _ since after _ the nights come dark, this house is very big and listen powerful noises on the outside; already almost when it's midnight, just thinking every day at night _ I start to have panic attacks, and _ sky turns _ dark because it is not moon full, at about eight o'clock at night it turns off the motor that generates electricity and everything Is left over dark only the support of the candles, it is here one of the differences of the town to this farm. The dark It really causes me panic and the worst only with my baby in this great country house.

how innocent or ambitious went to fall in love with Esteban, feeling that I am living a well- marked punishment, now I do not want any free penny given away, now learned to value things so insignificant _ but may they give happiness, with my mother and grandmother I really was a millionaire of love and peace with them, what a sadness who could imagine that by marrying me our matrimony life broke.

The dream life of love and peace never arrive, now I'm living a hell; and my baby does not have not even the thousandth fault, now I will fight by change it all but really to what price and to where I will arrive with Esteban, and my daughter, what else things terrible us wait, neither want to neither think about it better I'd like sleep but I also can't the nerves do not leave me sleep now _ Yeah there would be a price by sleep would pay but I can't neither paying for it what _ I have done bad to deserve this life ; the worst I don't know why how long time I have to waiting.?

Now with my husband's absence, since Peggy was born, Esteban, has left the farm since she was born, she hardly comes back, for a good part for me since the fights have ceased, but now the loneliness that

I feel in this house, I miss my family my sisters, this house me does feel bad, feel that I will become crazy.

every day in this house is a change to my person now I'm feeling sensations that I did not notice before such as in moment I feel that it hurts me he body, noises such as Yeah someone further apart from us this at home.

The only way that calms me down and helps me control he fear is taking in my arms my baby and I accommodated her close to my chest to feel that force by live.

But as soon as I'm calm and simultaneously I start other time listening to footsteps in the room, whistles, some object that falls to the ground, everything this is starting to get me tense .

my nerves are breaking down, now at night _ any noise I hear coming from outside gives me chills creepy that get me to the core .

With only the simple innocent buzz of the crickets scare me, the bright ones nocturnal fireflies hidden inside the grass gives me a strange sensation when observing them flashing their lights.

I'm scared _ the nerves make me hear things that may not exist _ _ nerves are getting me out of control, loneliness in this house, my family don't knew the hell what I am living with Esteban but I can't say nothing to avoid them problems with my husband .

Now it's a challenge everything scares me even wonderful worm colors _ giving radiance phosphorescent me they scare and the worst see any snake around, everything in the field is already putting up paranoid.

loneliness mortifying me maybe I miss my mom, granny and

siblings, how will they be happening, I was a selfish in the way that abandoned them and now here is my punishment living in a martyrdom caused by this husband inconsequential.

Need move since my concern little by little can affect my daughter, although this too much tender to understand my worries and sadness; neither must wait further time living in this farm; tomorrow will best ideas.

today is august ten, I am fulfilling nine months of marriage and my daughter two months of birth, nine months of sadness, loneliness what life is for me touching, I know that one exit I will have, but when will it be ? will it be I shall have further patience than I have until today?

He has not taken a little time to be with us and make life a little more enjoyable. As long as happens he time our relationship is being dying, his life is your friends, the liquor and girlfriends, which causes me only in think sadness, fatigue, desire to sleep crying, I feel devastated, betrayed, and what makes me living is my daughter

Today my ideas indicate that my escape from the farm is almost close to being done Actually, I hope that now my idea is safe, nor had _ imagined but something direct came to my mind ;

"MY MOTHER-IN-LAW CELIA, SHE CAN HELP ME." Yeah, yeah, she's the only one who can convince his _ son, to move at the San Felipe Town, since it would be better for the Baby girl by further security in case she gets sick, I am sure she'll convince him, I know Celia is so happy with the baby, since they have said that Peggy, is her portrait. Maybe would not like to spend a experience how did it happen at birth his granddaughter Peggy..

Something tells me this plan will work with Celia, anyway. I lose nothing by trying she will be happy proud by birth of his favorite granddaughter, about her even her mole _ it seems that it is his daughter.

today has been the day more happy for me, because the ideas are leaving very clear, I'm sure it will work, since we married Esteban, it's my first day that I filling happy already it seems that everything working well with move to town. but something tells me yes it will work I had not _ happened with so many worries that neither there was paying attention that Peggy, my little girl, is a miniature version of my mother-in-law, my little girl It will be the one that will help change my life a little,

I will try Tomorrow; in make my perfect plan. to escape far away from here together with my daughter.

Tomorrow I will determine my plan, and happy I headed to the kitchen very smilingly, I prepared one cup coffee and I began to savor it, felt so delicious, I feeling that life returned to my soul I repeated several times sipping my coffee saying I know my mother in law will accept that I move to town, for supposed I wouldn't like it either live in the mother in law house. But my mind imposed the doubt by second, saying what if my plan doesn't work what if she doesn't want me to move from this farm. No, it can't be, I have to be positive, she accept my proposal, I'm sure.

Well my decision is done, at the early morning I going in look for Mr. Efrain, since He gets up early to work, that fine is time to go sleep because tomorrow need get up early. so great that nothing to interrupt my thoughts, therefore I will go to the room to prepare my baby ready to sleep, talking very happy with my baby telling, her daughter tomorrow you will see you granny. You are so similar to her, with the difference she older and you a baby girl.

Well my sweet baby, we need get up early morning now is time to sleep.

Today I feel happy until could appreciate a very fresh day, with a rising sun, it seems that nature also smile with me, today I feel like the woman very happy.

Well Tula, time to stop talking by myself don't expend you time, and hastened my steps and left straight to the stable and precisely over there I found the butler Good morning Mr. Efrain, how are you?, He answered me, very good Mrs. Tula, they handshake saying Mt Efrain, it's very early is not usual you around here, I think what you have something in special to telling me. I am here, me Tula with little smiling saying of course. Yes you are right, I need you help I would like you to have preparer an beast around eleven in the morning, I will take a little trip to town with my mother-in-law and I would like take them some little gifts; she likes tortillas made _ _ for Tomasita, and I would like you to prepare new beans, fresh and dry curds. I know my mother-in-law love eat those. Efrain answered, don't worry, at eleven will be Ready the filly with the two saddlebags.

on my way could to appreciate Mrs. Tomasita, coming with two buckets for the milk, saying Her, hello so happily she made comment for my good mood, since you, always _ path by the surroundings very sad, and now look very smiling, yes Tomasita you right most sad and crying, but today it's because today something good happen me, for now!.

still talking and Handshake then Tula say see you late Tomasita, Mr. Efrain will telling you my happiness.

At exactly ELEVEN IN THE MORNING, the butler was already waiting for me with my orders, and I marveled since the beast was the one I like much the most elegant white mare with its spots black in circles. Over there were the butler and Tomasita waiting to help me with the girl went out quickly with the baby in Arms, gave Her to Tomasita, to be able to me ride the mare, my orders already next to the packsaddle, with a little effort since I was not accustomed, then I sit down on the beast, when safety, Tomasita bring my little girl.

The mare seemed to understand _ all the time ready to get the way, this galloped very slowly It seemed that understood that I have my baby on my arm. Since felt the march very slow; the trotting of this mare makes me safety. At first time I was a little afraid of falling, but I went reassuring in the way that really felt it very short. Little by little we are entering the town until reached my mother-in-law's house.

Well Until here starting felting uncomfortable since I needed help, the only action it is stop from the door saying Hello, is there anyone at home, someone may help me please? I started calling to Matilde employee, but no one answered my requesting, for two minutes stop in requesting help, then still again saying open the door please am Tula, I am on the mare and I have my baby in my arms I need help sooner, since some minutes door suddenly opened to my surprise it was not the employee who opened the door, their appeared my mother-in-law with a big smile with the look rigid towards his granddaughter and how could achievement take in his arms to the baby girl, telling them a number of adorable phrases, touching their cheeks with a sweet tone of voice, saying, how beautiful my sweetheart looks a porcelain doll; my mother-in-law was so excited that she ignored me all his attention was only focused to me Peggy.

Celia did not stop in tell him things beautiful my little doll this already growing up, and the baby such he seemed to understand what she saying his grandmother, only remained seeing Celia about to smile at Her.

I dismounted from the horse, there was Matilde arrived, and took the mare by the reins, to the place where the beasts are tied.

no comment We entered the house, and when we were both comfortably taking advantage of how excited my mother-in- law was, by the arrival of her little granddaughter don't hesitate in Ask, Celia, have you seen Esteban? She stayed _ very quiet such as Yeah I ignore my question, and continued she saying sweet words to the baby, for the moment she make pause saying I haven't seen Him, but I think He is continues submerged in getting drunk on liquor therefore better not to talk about Him. Tula, did not comment about your _ husband, and they talked about things from the live in town, after a few breaks I was directly with my mother-in-law, explaining the plan to move from the farm to the Town, telling her my concerns and the because I owe myself leave the farm, since I don't have support with Him, if my baby have a medico emergency, it is very hard for me go out in a hurry at night _ Looking for a doctor, you know I don't have any Esteban's support, that why only you would like to help me doing possible my move, otherwise I will escape with my baby, well I have to watch over she whatever it takes .

My mother in law stayed quietly by some moments _ no comment; and continued focused in the attention of the baby girl.

Celia responds to Tula's concern by telling her, no worry I will see how to talk with Esteban and also try to convince my husband, quiet for minutes Celia, telling to Tula, don't desperate, back to the farm and waiting probably next week you will have a hello with good news, because my granddaughter can't continue living in the field, she deserves a life better. When listening those words for part of mother-in-law, my heart be excited

I spend the week and such as She was promised Celia, that in the next week would have news about it, and what was promised is a debt, Esteban appeared giving me the good news of moving to the Town, saying it would be good for our family . when i was saying good _ I said to myself, shouting alone, thanks to my Virgin Mary who is in my life my plan to help worked, it worked, that's good.

Chapter # 9

TULA AND PEGGY BACK TO SAN FELIPE TOWN

It seems that really Esteban, no wanted to live on the farm and the news in quotes made him feel happy, his father Francisco approved that they should move to the town, giving him orders my husband to go see Maurito who seems to be selling one of his houses.

Esteban, don't wait, went to Maurito's house to put in I treat the house that was in sale, without hesitation they made the deal on the fifth of November, putting dates to buy the house staying in contract for November 20, after the meeting Esteban, going in fact to bring the good _ notice to Tula with the exact date of the purchase of the new house, already Could say that it's sure the move to town.

For a few days stopped talking myself, my happiness was immense, but I was trying to hide a bit since I was afraid that Esteban would suspect that it was all my plan to move to the Town, and it was afraid that He would change his mind and don't like to move, it's Going well, only expect.

The deal was made on the date indicated, one day before departure I started to pack the little clothes we had, a once finished I left _ lay down very happy closed my eyes such as Yeah was asleep, as usual my husband arrive late I was asleep, well I was afraid that He would notice my Immense joy and very moved because the house we were buying It was a block and a half away from my family.

Up to this point no longer made myself illusions with keeping our marriage, for all the beatings that Esteban has given me, really I have fear and what matters to me is having further secure my daughter 's health . On the farm my girl was in danger of being bitten by an insect weird, snake and more, really on the farm was turning me a paranoid especially at night, made felt scares around me,

In reality I was not prepared to live in a farm alone, be away from my family, also realized how much missed my mother, Grandmother and siblings,

Have my daughter was a gift from God. My baby is just what I wanted.

During my pregnancy, I prayed to God and Virgin Mary to bless me with a baby healthy. I asked him that my girl did not have none malformation physics, I was terrified lose her after the beating that gave my alcoholic husband.

didn't expect a girl so pretty at birth and then she left forming a lovely baby, golden and curly hair, skin white, nose fine, eyes of honey, it seems a little doll

I'm immensely happy to move to Pueblo San Felipe, but now I wonder what of our future? Living in a new home, Esteban has not changed go on alkalized; which will be our lives I really can't feel a good feeling that comes from Him, he doesn't take care about my daughter and me now we are moving grace to my mother-in-law She doing everything for love of her granddaughter. For a better place moving to the town San Felipe.

Chapter # 10

SADNESSES OF PEGGY AND TULA

Tula thinking about her daughter saying; So long it's been six years what my Peggy was born, and Esteban still ingesting liquor, We are in the house as us my parents in-laws bought, we are live with the little that our in laws give us to feed my girl, also my mother help with little food and money

My mother telling me, have careful in take care in not more pregnant she bothers for not take care for that.

now she bring some contraceptives. But Esteban, throw it in the garbage, because him not like me take pill to prevent pregnancies.

I don't know that can do with my matrimony nothing working in my life.

I'm young but I don't feeling that way, I feel old, and sad lady.

I'm watching in get divorce, leave away, but my thoughts are vague, since I have no financial base to survive with my three daughters, I need support, someone help me in my plans, I need see the other way time to escape but need support, something to get me out of this violence, necessary a chance to escape .

my family can't do nothing have you fear of my husband 's aggressiveness .

Today went to registered Peggy, at school, already fulfilled seven years of age, and the next year begin to his class, I hope the school will help her at least she has their friends to play and develop as such .

Now as It could be the life of Peggy, everything this to be seen, but something tells me that not expect nothing good with my husband.

Really it was a miracle leaves the farm, though since Peggy, was born, Esteban forgot that we needed food, clothes and about all comprehension by hence love.

Now my life has turned into hell, girls are growing and very scared, very difficult for them understand our situation in our house. With an alcoholic parent.

Never imagined that I was marrying an abuser, the worst thing that we do not have support by part of Esteban, and my in-laws ignore everything that we happens, but they do not have any plan to help us, our life it is disaster my family they really have him fear, the authorities ignore our complaints, how far reach this?

The childhood they are carrying my daughters, ruled for domestic violence by an irresponsible _ husband alcoholic.

Tula make a little commitment about her daughter saying my Peggy, has so much sweetness, since I was three years old, had a great feeling by me, to his age showed so much love,

Especially when me, sick, could see his effort that she made by bring me a glass of water. Could notice his worry she ran to take a chair and with a lot effort achieved bring me water, in Peggy could _ see the tenderness for me.

She always look sadness just to see me most of the times crying, fighting with my husband; so strong, I have no words to express how sad my heart is, struggling by do something to leaving this torment life.

Peggy have a little conversation with me Tula, but it made me felt more sad because she said, Mon, is impossible not to be here when been in class, am afraid that my father would kill you, very difficult much pain to see you beatings from my dad, Mother, every blow that my Dad gave you, I felt it, my heart hurt and I could not do anything.

Me, Peggy, tell her Mon again I'll waiting for have and living in peace.

Nobody calm my pain see you mother being beaten for my Dad. Really sad the screams of my siblings, and me yelled until stayed exhaust hoarse _ and nobody came to help, feared losing you Mon, final end the fainting, siblings and me with you Mon to cure the heal the wounds and clean the blood on his body; mom is life it. When we go far away.

Every day felt like losing the hope of protecting my mother, I screamed, asking outside by looking to see someone coming to help, sad, because no one coming to help us, terrible pain.in that time don't understanding why the people in this Town shut the doors when they heir our screams, sad?

The neighbors us they were unaware, they did not have compassion by us, and the worst after each _ fight my Dad left home as calm as who says here nothing has happened, while we trying to heal the wounds of you mon,

Really what body you Mon very strong to support endure, wounds with hand weapons, blows.

We were so small children and powerless to such violence domestic, the aggressive fights happened on weekends, my sisters many times they yelled at exhaustion and others occasions they hid behind the doors.

I felt so much love for you mother, I don't anything to spoil you, I love Mon

I wanted heaven blue just for seeing happy, wish many gifts all the best in the world. But nothing, you always look sad I wish you hug me and tell me things pretty, but I understood you.

Leave alone to my dad and go far from here.

to ease our sorrows in which we lived mon.

Today is "MOTHER" day. looked you with much tenderly, I wished hug, you not gave that opportunity, also why you never hug me or kiss me but the desire to hug you is strong. but only stay to see you face.

Today is MOTHER DAY. The time that well living with my drunken father? My Mon doesn't know the mother day celebration.

I don't forget those days when my father was away for days, I remember that in the distance she doing the trades home, and me _ well sit observing her long, want hug and kiss her, but I can't do it because she never do that. Love mon you are my angel.

She living to waiting for the time then my Dad coming home,, since I remember that many times She move our bed said get up his father comes very drunk let's go running now. can imagine with what time she will give us good attention and well care for as? No my father did not allow it, all alert in take care for the time when my Dad coming home, if him coming drinking will going outside until him sleept or back to the street.

He was the most selfish.

There was a moment when I thought what my Mon. was a women very cold as a rock, the pain that She had felt forgotten, nobody supported Her, she defended herself how I could, I always looked at her doing their trades very pensive such like only her existed in the kitchen, She forgot that there we were watching her Really I wished that really only us we were at her side, but not my father.

When memory those days so terrible, impossible control my tears, but it also made me difficult understand my mother, because she losing the feeling of the love for us well also we needed heir a sweetheart from Mon, I never remember in giving me a hug, on my birthdays, Christmas

, I do not deny in Christmas we had our Christmas gifts, but all simple without that darling that it felt that heat human of love, we were creating without that heat human, I felt that yes I needed a little hug, a little kiss in the cheek. _

Now Peggy make a little comemment by herself asking so sad, wonder because my mother is so cold, it will be that she does not have that tenderness of mother, that feeling turned see her cold like a rock any way I know that love Her I want to hug and tell mother I love a lot. why she so cold with me.

Always admired her despite her coldness, actually recognize she like a bird than bought food bring it in the nest then feed all babies birds. never lacked food, and she was everything to me, at Christmas _ us commanded early to sleep since Santa Claus would arrive with gifts. But never us gave a hug at dawn at Christmas _ over there we had our gifts were only in those days that my parents did not do conflicts at home, for that always think that my father did not love Mama, because at Christmas he did not do no conflict, the month of December we had a good time, like children, happy playing with their new toys

Chapter # 11

ABUSE AND TEARS

Peggy, commandment Never could to understand why dad, hat deals always to my mother with so much cruelty? It seemed that my mother had his eye bandaged; I wonder why doesn't he run away? Because wait by beating that one day he could kill Her. I won't forgive to my dad, that neither in the day of his funeral.

To this day why so much mistreatment to my mon, the Town of San Felipe was witness of our misfortunes lived there.

That pain frames our lives, those memory they will live until and after death.

Chapter # 12

CHANGED HIS LIFE BY LIQUOR

Peggy still make commitment just memories disgusting my parents had left in my mind, those days of mistreatment towards my mother Tula, with knives, guns, punches, even stones . Sometimes we went out running from home to seek help. _

Our neighbors us they were closed their doors, and we as crazy in a hurry in the street desperate, disconsolate in not finding aid in our neighbors, quickly and very sad we returned home thinking in the worst that could happen to my mother .

Sometimes the fight there was finished and my father's aggressor had already disappeared like a bad spirit.

Many times we found sitting my mother healing her wounds, alone bloody, and we helping her, and we are sad because there was no not one to Protect us, my grandparents quiet, still knowing what we was happening, to our age could not understand why _ no nobody try to help us ?

He hit her so hard rage, such that he wanted kill her, always my mother was trying to defend himself but always she came out bloodied, it broke him his nose, hit her very ugly. was ours panic see blood by all living room.

He's went quit from the house and still taking liquor with their friends, they also were bad guy, for not avoiding my mom mistreat..

I always asked to my mon, why don't we escaped, we need go far away, why bear so much, please mom, didn't say we can't because, he always us will find and be worse he punishment for me, Mon, the life here is so sad, let go far from this town.

I am filing so stress because we are invisible in this San Felipe Town.. Our life is sad,

I realized that she everything did _ in bear it for love of us, for fear of not having as give al care to us.

Chapter # 13

LIQUEUR MAKE HIM A
FURIOUS MONSTER

Most of the times Tula made detail him when came drunk, sometimes by surprise and it is when we could not escape, then my father like crazy threw my mother all the objects that he found mercilessly, he broke his head to my mother while my little sisters They ran to hide, while me stayed _ over there screamed telling Him, to stop, looking for something to defend my mother, most of the time could throwing the broom, but made felt nervous and blind, nothing looked around and what could do? I am a little girl with the only attempt to stop the violence but was in vain.

my father was a monster enraged after the fight as always, we would approach my mother and hug her how to give cheer up, I felt exhausted, tired, in the fight to protected to my mother, was over, and stayed hoarse, from screaming so much it was my way of defending my mother, thinking that he would listen to me, but nothing my screams carry by the wind. Sadness, pain, hard time for me.

This is our true reality, for being my MOTHER of poor recourse economic; it Made her invisible in that Town San Felipe.

My mother a women young unfortunately lived in a situation unfortunate, its sad reality.

For my Mother, sisters, and me; our lives were marked in that town, they know my father's mistreatment against my mother; and no one made anything for her.

My father was of one of the son of parent's rich people from San Felipe, but we lived in a miserable life.

Today has been a fight so hard, wish someone _ us protect me from my father's fury, this day I thought my mother would not bear other beatings, since I saw that the fight started, I ran toward the command, pass in a hurry in front of my grandparents' house; I just took a look without stopping running like a crazy, to the police station. The distance between my home and police station was almost ten blocks, the

Finally arrived at the Police station,, there several officer, between few words since the tiredness did not allow me speak well and I told them, run my mother need help because my father is killing to my mother, they did not put attention to my pain, and only told me come back, already let's go to your house in few minutes be there in instantly realized that they were not putting up attention to my appeal, to my short age could understand the indifference they were misleading me they would not go to protect my mother; turned around and returned the same way, when arrived home I felt fainting, from the exhaustion of running, I knew that I had no time to stop I had to run, to arrive on time and see that my mother was not there dead.

This day remains in my mind by all my life, at my early age could know, that the poor are worth nothing to the rich. Nobody in town didn't anything to make stop to my dad, despite being a drunken abuser hitting ruthlessly to his wife,

And despite all those bad things happen in our life, to my short age came many ideas to my mind; when all passed, stayed with the desires in return to the of San Felipe, Town and ask why? Why didn't they mate my father? but in my mind stay the pain of mistreatment to my mother, and the indifference of the authorities and our neighbors, most the neighbors were family, there were no entities could help Mon. that were called guards, police, there were no friends, there were no neighbors, we were like as ghosts ignored. Many times I wondered where my father's family to help us, my grandmother Celia where was? They living arrow four block to my home, they forgot about us.

If one of my grandparents would have called the authorities, they would have heard, but never had we had that protection.

How sad for us; why the parents of my Dad, don't protected us, we were ignored for them and from the people in the town.

The neighbors closed their doors and I wonder how far their indifferences they ignore our pain, it would be that their ears got used to hear our pain? I swore like that same as in my life I will not allow I mistreat myself and children .My father did not hit but yes to my mother, saw that it is lake hurt we, it not only caused me anguish, I could also feel the pain he's made to my mother.

I had seven years old and the violence domestic not end, in my mind the sad moments when my little sisters when they seeing my Dad come home, they ran to hiding, behind the doors, listening, and cried; and they can't do nothing for my mother, while me, screaming uncontrollably in waiting for a neighbor come to help as, but no one came to our house in help.

Most of the time my mother stretched on the floor bleeding; then the aggressor of my Dad leaves the home like the party end here, and nothing happen.

But I cannot believe the incredibly resistance of my mother, really don't know.

Many times I went out with my little sisters and we ran on the street asking for helped, and no one appeared to help, my little sisters ran with their tears falling down on their cheeks, inconsolable we were returning quickly to see my mother and hope still alive.

When returning home we saw him out control fiercely so demonized that also wanted to kill us, looking for stone and threw to kill us, to the point that he knocked down one those of my sisters Alexandrina, she fell to the ground his blood ran by his small face, it was the last thing I remember.

Always felt adulthood, childhood did not cross my mind at all, as a result of this incident, I begged my mother telling we going to other place, I have afraid of losing you, but my mother did not give me none answer positive, there continued, and we too.

Now I wonder it is love that she feels by Him? Maybe she thinks that one day it will change, I really don't think so? The situation it is crossing the limits; which will be our destination?

Already I'm tired, I no longer have the head to think in other place; just waiting for the next one fight to come, I am resigned to the worst.

I have always wondered and one day I will have a conversation with my father. When will it be? I will ask him why so much hate against to my mother? Just thinking what happens if my mother died? What would become of us, we would stay abandoned, just thinking in this dramatic situation my eyes fill with tears. _

I don't finish in ask me because so much violence, why He not had a little bit of tenderness? One day I would like visit that Town, and more than one person will tell me why they not defended us from my father's abuse. Why the people from that San Felipe Town not were friendly with us, like good people.

Worry why the neighbors not we defended from my father's violence? The neighbors never could call the Police? Why didn't they do it? Already as adult I will returned to the town of SAN FELIPE to investigate the reason from the indifference.

I'm sure there are still people who knew our story, with my parent, an alcoholic abuser against to my Mon.

Chapter # 14

FACE TO FACE WITH MY DAD

Peggy knew who her dad, was many time sarcastic with her, but she also had the guts to tell her dad truth el her dad

Were few times what was talking face to face with my Dad, and it just happened in the few times that he was sober . In the time sober it was shown that really we were a normal family; it pleased me to sit with him to eat, with only one day, I could feel an eternity of peace, such it seemed that there would be no further fight.

One day of many we were together at lunchtime waiting for my mother served the food, we are sitting opposite each other, I felt happy to see it, such he seemed like a good man and me little girl just want play and live in peace, there as always my Dad, toward some jokes, good at those moments my Mon served the food, a fried chicken that tasted very good, ate all the little chicken bones soft from my plate, then asked my Dad, for his chicken bone.

I wonder with a countenance very serious, telling me why you eat bones? eat only the chicken and not the bone, telling I not gave you the bone because bone it's food for the dog.

Minutes after my mother appeared and my Dad with

sarcastically very seriously said; Tula, today night Peggy, will sleep under the bed she go sleep with the dogs because already she eats bones, when Dad, finish to talk, I started to cry, had resentful sleep under the bed, felt very ugly, because I liked eat little bones, really would be the first time we ate together, I remember that time and not forget, but I still eating chicken bones are delicious, but it wasn't such a big deal that I slept with the dogs, I felt also a little dog, and thought that He was so rude with me, well never told me don't worry about the bone,, he just remained so calm, without thinking that he made feel bad.

Chapter # 15

PROVOKING MY DAD TO
MAKE HIM ANGRY

Peggy stil with hard story around her parents. I do not deny that there were days of peace in our home, days are numbered, nothing more, but I ca not forget some incidents that happened in my childhood life, remember cause me laugh.

It was approximately four in the afternoon, my Dad, was in the patio in the part back of the house sitting on that big old tree fallen on the patio, many times it served as a big seat for conversation. Over there saw my Dad was sit sharpening a knife, look like a man sober a family man very jovial I went to him, and sat down at a distance of one meter, and by some minutes began to observe Him, to seeing what He doing .

I made sure MY FATHER was sober, also saw him that he was relaxed sharpening a knife,

Like as all unmeasured girl with none consequence, a little sarcastically said Dad,

YOU WERE ARRESTED ON SATURDAY?

"He answered me without little shame; yes
* DAD WAS ME, WHO CALLED THE GUARD. THE ONLY WAY FOR THEM TO TAKE ATTENTION OF ME WAS TO MAKE LIES TO THEM; I TOLD THEM THAT YOU WANTED TO TALK TO THEM VERY URGENTLY.*

THEY COULD HAVE PROVED THAT YOU WERE MISTREATING MY MOTHER.
Dad, you have to understand what since today I am capable of defending my mother. Hearing what I did in second he lost his cool, he looked at me and yelled at me furiously said little girl, now you are see WHAT I WILL DO, Quickly put his hands on his belt, I stayed there for some seconds seeing what he doing.

Well my mind thinks fast; I need moved because, he would punish would be gave me merciless lashes, but he don't know that I am a gazelle to run, already I am accustomed with his fights with my mother, running was my defense, well knowing what awaited me I ran towards the street, after that I don't remember anything if he me reached me or no.

That conversation was in private between my Dad and me; also not tell anything above to my Mon. think with that conversation was _ implying that I am ready to protect my mother.

I was no longer the girl of five or six, anymore now I have seven years old, the beatings of domestic violence, that him cause to my mother, those were awakening my innocence

Chapter # 16

SURPRISE TO MY DAD

Peggy with more surprise to her Dad, She defends her mother from the ingratitude of her dad.

In this issue they will think that I am a girl naughty, but what don't understood that I could no longer see My Dad, close to my mother, he bothered me, had to be there, the domestic violence is changing my feelings for my father, I am losing the respectful toward him, also he fear, I got to the point that what I wanted to go far away together with mon, and my siblings. I had already very tired no more fights.

Saturday afternoon when my Dad appeared very sober and friendly; telling me, start watering the little plants in the garden, me very obedient and sisters we seek the utensils for watering, I bucket further big, but first my father asked where you mother? We answered she, in the room and we left running to bring water. He would be there waiting for us to help us water,

And ready to bring he water and us we went, return with him water, my father was not there, quickly without putting he bucket of water I went to the living room and He is not there, I went quick to the room there were both very sheltered with the sheet,, I got angry a lot and throw them over the bucket of water cold.

I stayed over there by some second to see that passing by, suddenly saw how quickly my DAD THROWED THE SHEET, at that moment I needed wings to fly, and as usual I left as room gazelle, non - stop take a look toward behind and not believe it, there My DAD was coming, behind me . His EYES red like a tomato VERY BRAVE, and the chase as he cat to mouse,

I got a little distracted and Him, hunt me, LIKE THE CAT REACH THE MOUSE, He took me to home, there my mother and my sisters did not dare to defend me I knew what there waiting for me a beating; it would be the first that my Dad, would give me, because never had me punished, he only hit my mother.

As could I let go of his hands and another time and ran over the river ravine.

I fell when back home already _ _ near the house.my father caught me with one hand and grabbed me strongly thinking that I could escape and with the other hand unbuttoned his belt I had afraid he would beating me with his belt, it was wide and made of pure leather with animal designs, I a little girl very skinny, neither imagine the beating, he began to litigate me, over and over time, I already felt that I was dying when suddenly I heard my mother say, no more this is the first and last time you hit one of my daughters, never you will mistreat them; any of my children. Never any finger on them, does it with me, but not with them, and He, stop hitting.

My mother took me in his arms and back home. Ached all my body _

I really don't know if I deserved a punishment like that an aggressive drunk, but that day he was very sober, but his anger was immense.

for me was the beating unforgettable, every time remember it saw myself in the scenes it makes me sad, don't remember the days I waited to heal my wounds from girdles _

Whenever I remember standing in front of his bed with a bucket of water, and remember only beating that my father gave me, and just imagining he bucket with water cold over them and the worst in bed, when reminded me of that incident and caused me laugh, just how I throw them the bucket of cold water, it may be that I deserved such a brutal punishment, in my opinion I think no, because lied, he would wait in the garden waiting for the water.

Very good "THAT WAS THE GREAT SURPRISE FOR MY FATHER, I NEVER HAD IMAGINED GIVING HIM A SURPRISE OF THAT NATURE.

But now that I write it, I live reality and tears come to my eyes imagining the beating he gave me.

I could never imagine throwing a bucket of water at them cold. I did not measure the consequences, the bed got wet, and Tula, did not imagine the magnitude of the punishment.

Chapter # 17

PANIC IN AN EARLY MORNING

Peggy still slept,

Early morning, my mother with very quietly movement woke up us from our pleasant and deep sleep, he told me I wait for you behind the house; Get up, Esteban already arriving drunk with his friends.

The panic _ us put on quickly on our feet, we were scared, listening several men's voices, arrive home, is me Dad, with his Alcoholic drunk friends, I heard his voice, fast get up, telling to my little sisters in a hurry before the fight starts, there was no finished saying fight when litter sister up, I took them by their hands and we left quietly.

We got to the back house, their our mother waiting for us with some sheets, and we half sleepy, we went to a neighbor house we knock on the door we were sure they open but the unfortunately don't opened the door and we go to hide in a mountainous place known to my Mon.

How could my mother did he path cutting up little branches with his hand and conditioning the place putting the on the floor a blanket make a comfortable for us; all it was fine as long as we didn't witness our parents fights. Over there we felt a perfect hiding the place he lent himself to hide us, there us we sit quietly watching us each other _ while my mother began to pray it was still very dark, since there was no dawned completely, something happen good it still the moon was there and it was shining our way, that we could see by where we were walking protecting us from snakes and other animals poisonous, such It seemed that our God was listening to my mother 's prayers .

I'm sure an angel us protected since in a tropical place there are insect vipers especially in _ the area a lot of rattle snakes and corals, really don't remember any picket,. God was really with us over there we will return home maybe they already left, we prepared to return, and it was a fact they had gone, we arrive to home. Quickly we headed to the room to continue sleeping.

The next day, my mother asked me to accompany her to the river and we stopped by some moments exactly by the place where we were state hidden last night, since I couldn't believe that we were state in that place; were there looked so protected, it seemed a true cave covered with branches green than us toward feel us protected, today is not what we had seen the night before.

Right now I'm seeing a bramble of thorns not the same at the last night. I wonder it was a miracle to find a good refuge.

My mother and me were safe that we been there, it was unmistakable since the moon illuminated very radiant, the good thing that whenever we went out in escape, any Hideaway was perfect for us.

I'm fine Convinced that our God listens my mother's prayers to helped; that we let's feel protected in that hideout.

Chapter # 18

ANOTHER DRUNK DAY

Tula commenment her sad life.

What to do between whispers said my mon again comes intoxicated, it would be seven at night, shouting where are you Tula, my Mon, respond I'm here what do you want?, go to buy a bottle liquor, strong that burns me throat, my mother obediently he answered yes and took _ a bottle empty of liquor, quickly my mother enter our room saying get up we have to go. Like usual quickly us we get up and carefully that do not see Dad.

This time we did not know where ask for lodging, in he I walk my mother us indicated where _ we would go, and it was a place that never we had asked for a posada, there your Dad will be not look for as.

Well says Tula it time, we need going with my cousin Daniel's house, his house was a block from ours home, but let us said never we went to Mama's family house, to avoid problems with Dad, we arrived at my mother's relative's house, I knocked on the door and right away they opened the door, well the whole family knew our sadness with the violence and abuser of our father toward my mon.

Kindly us received the lady Ninfa mother of Daniel, very kindly us He let us in, we entered and without questions us they showed a room small and very dark, but the fear did not exist for us, it was just a room dark it's normal in our life, the most important thing have refugee out of danger.

When we left the house, my dad stayed deceived, since mon, did not return with the bottle of liquor.

was no past an hour when from our hiding place we could hear their screams and as pulled the furniture; very quietly listened the scandalous make in our house for my Dad, no way to go home.

in the morning next, I got up happy in the cousin's house because I give a good news to my little sisters, about the conversation then I had with mon, finally we will leave San Felipe, we we'll go to live with aunt Cruz, today my mother will talk with her for lodging help us, if we will go to Managua, there our father will not allow him.

My mother came up telling us, we have to go home, listening to her us it was nice then I felt hungry my little simblis also,

We went home but am I way thought in mon, finally she is thinking well, maybe she is tired of beatings and also me, I'm tired, I don't know anymore that do for her to leave PAPA, now what matters is that mom is out of danger, no more _ abuse to Her .

Chapter # 19

GUN IN HAND

Rifle in hand, the panic was so strong seeing my father with weapons, too the knives scare me. _

my poor mother thinking that she was free and that she could do any think what she estimate convenient, in a sunset maybe to get us out of the routine in which we lived, we He said we would take a walk and visit his Aunt Amalia, she lived about two blocks from our house, she have small business of making bread and tortillas to selling..

Well we went to Aunt Amalia's house, such It seemed that day would be peaceful, she us received very kindly us we sat together with MOM, they began to talk.

Sooner we hear on the outside someone very angry, neither by our mind we would think the person is our father, and really was him very furious looking for us, like a furious lion, He do not enter the house but was acting as demon with his rifle in hand started calling us by age order _ and we went Leaving Aunt Amalia 's house .

First call to MAMA, then my little sister minor Alexandrine, then Denise, and lastly me. I was the last in line, really we had panic, we thought that that day we would die, we were lined up; my father went to the end of the line and ordered authoritatively walk._

we felt as hostages my mother look in shock, very calm and in silence obeyed him I think that she thought we were arrive the day of dying.

my mother could not believe how far your _ Husband, has come with his abuses, could notice mom's face reflected fear also had panic, this time my mother was in disadvantage did not have option only remains to fallow order from my Dad. This day my MOM was very intelligent cautious with her performance at this point we did not know dad intentions, perhaps it was a provocation I think so she would have resisted maybe us would have shot.

that day has been unforgettable for me, when I remember I see myself walking home, in a guard line and my father behind us, I remember Excitedly, the time was approximately three in the afternoon, we walked the two blocks to the house, the neighbors did look at each other but I'm sure they were spying from somewhere in their homes.

we were walking scared, that was other scene that I will never forget, which I really can't remember nothing at all what happened when we got home, not really I remember nothing when arrive to our home.

Chapter # 20

CUT THE KNOT

Tula, still relating her life during marriage with Esteban.

my life does not have sense, what is in mon head, another baby and the situation does not improve, now nobody the understand, what body can resist so much mistreatment, at my early age would not bear it .

My mother has given birth to another baby and he is a boy, and my father named Esteban JR, now that we wait the escape it was planned by my mother but it is gone; we not have hope.

I feel that we are destined for martyrdom, now it's only my turn accept what we have.

Esteban Jr. was born in August six, and today has exactly two months today is October 6, this day my father is sober and looks very relaxed, such like nothing bothers him, and that's good, my mother this in the kitchen preparing a chicken, and he baby sleeping in the room in a hammock, here I am taking care of newborn, at the moment I saw my dad, walk quietly in direction of the new baby boy with a knife, for now I look at it cutting the ropes of the hammock, with my eyes wide open and surprised, I stayed paralyzed without doing anything, didn't know that do, what was seeing I did not have comparison . But mother's intuition that something was wrong, some feeling she felt that I suddenly saw her enter the room, I was over there witnessing the terrible act that was doing my father, when suddenly my mon, coming and seeing to my Dad aggressively asking telling him What's you doing to my baby.

As a dog rabid and fair with reason said Him, what are you going to kill my baby? I not allow it hanging from the rope of the hammock, the baby fallen over them, miraculously was unharmed, and can't able to take him in my arms, while my Dad, mercilessly beat my mother.

This time the fight was completely different from the others; my father was already leaving my Mother ready to reach until the last consequences.

He quickly tied up the shoes and went out almost running from home, I understood that his intention was to provoke a fight and go with his friends to get drunk on liquor; He did not realize either account what already his marriage was reaching the limit of separation from his family.

But don't know that brought in mind that my mother was made of wood, and we invincible, so far I don't know that it will be in our lives. But I know that something will happen and this will finish.

Chapter # 21

PREPARING THE ESCAPE

Tula, and me Peggy, with our mind tormented looking for a way to make money and save to escape and forget about the domestic violence that we live with our father, the best idea my mother came up with is to sell tacos to our neighbors, typically he The best time to sell them is on Sundays. Some families don't like cook that day. Also thinking that our father would not interfere in our plan He usually appears in the afternoon or at night. _

My mon, very excited with the taco business, she went around the neighbors informing that the Sunday would have tacos and enchiladas for breakfast and lunch, for sale. My Mom without losing time she went to the village store to buy all the ingredients to use to prepare meals; did not take long a lot in go shopping and go back home .

She began to prepare the meat, and left all ready for food, the next day Sunday, she get up very early, my mother showed worried but didn't comment on it, I'm Thinking that as DAD, he didn't come to sleep: He's will show up at any moment, and our plan would collapse .

No shouldn't worry since my dad, usually arrive late the

Sundays, I couldn't believe were approximately eight in the morning, when my father appeared, going right way to the kitchen over there is my dad, telling Her, have ready my food, she kept looking by some moments and told him, not just wait the meat will be list in some minutes, my Mom, still close to the big pan full of pork meet, and my dad, ruthless, kicked the big pan of meat that was frying, and shut up falling on my mother 's_ towards their feet at the knees, crying loudly of pain were terrible the oil boiling ran by his legs and feet, sat on the ground agonizing of pain, she felt die. To see my Mon pain, my Dad, still as a coward heartless, without a bit of feeling neither Mercy, in saw my Mon pain I get the way running quickly look for help.

Finally the neighbors are deigned giving first aid to Mon,

It was able for the neighbors by the screams came from the terrifying scene cause for my dad.

They found her, in a puddle of blood and oil boiling, since with the metal of pan broke it cut his leg. They quickly helped her and called a nurse to heal her wounds and burns.

After that terrible violence _ neighbors turned further compassionate with my mother and with us, how much violence we have endured and so far a bit of sanity.

She healed; but the scars remained on his foot, the pain was so deep for me Peggy also my Mom never forget it. And my father cynically like nothing happens in his home.

He seems that has not awareness neither feeling, is a man who should not be my father.

very tiring for us try to defend my mother from the brutal fights that caused my FATHER, since little girl trying to search mechanisms to defend my mother, but my mechanism was crying and screaming and run by the street for help but back home without any Help, no one took pity on us .

May asking again? Wonder that strong my mother to hold on?

When she wounds healed, we continue waiting for the day of our escape, the neighborhood it started to support us, my mother did not lose the enthusiasm to prepare tacos and enchiladas, the neighbors us bought and we happy was not much money but we were saving we know one day will be leaf this town. SAN FELIPE.

Chapter # 22

KICKING MY GRAMMA

Around midnight hidden Esteban, in a dark night try to enter in GRANDMOTHER'S house, my granny us commented in detail, how He entered, no one saw Esteban inter to the home, that day he was sober, and was straight to my granny's room she, was sleeping deeply, he approached and grabbed her shoulders telling him, get up old hag: she how could got up and stood up, telling her, now get in under the bed, and she did such as requested, another _ time said now get out of there; for some minutes she state under bed, and my granny didn't come out. Him, yelled at her telling come out, since she didn't come out, he bent down and pulled her out of her hair, she I scream very loud by the pain it caused pulling her hair.

All side from her neighborhood heard the lamentations of my grandmother; the neighborhood around they were relatives some of them were grandmother nephews.

And they have so much estimation for her, they are young and strong, startled to hear the screams of my granny figured it was the Esteban savage, and they quickly headed to my Gramma house.

Nephew Pedro and Joaquin; but Pedro left quickly to Tula, house, to inform her what Esteban is hit her mother..

Tula woke up the girls and took them a neighbor to take care of them and she came home quickly, and before leaving the house look for a very sharp knife, Tula, have so much courage that no longer know what am capable to make, this is the last day of abuse that Esteban doing to my family, I can't anger control, my body shaking.

However luck is in my favor, I could no longer see the evil born of my husband, since the police had him taken under arrested, but my cousins tell me that before he was take for the police they gave him a beating, such like the anger that Esteban used against my mother.

How good they did me the favor since it would not be responsible for my actions when seeing it, this was the last drop that overflows he glass of water; it is already a fact of separating from Esteban. when my mother felt _ better, we taking in taking advantage of this temporarily arrested,

Tula comment, what her mother telling is time to take a stop to my relationship with Esteban. And my Grandma will taking with my sister Felicita who lived in the capital.

Look at the possibility to get temporary aid.

My grandma asks Tula, you sure won't come back? Because really don't want to see you with the same drama with you husband. Tula answered, mother tries to help me and I promise what I am end with my marriage.

If its fact meanwhile you take the baby and Peggy I'll stay with Denise and Mercy, when you filing comfortable, will give back the littler girls back you. Please you not have to return for the girls, we will be communicating and when the time I'll bring the girls is. .

Very good Mom, this is the last abuse that you receive from Esteban, I have to take advantage now He's in jail, Say Grandma, when He out from jail, you must be away from this neighborhood, I think he has received his abusive punishment _ I think that he will never set foot in my house again, go away peaceful daughter .

After having _ conversed with my mother. I said to myself, I think me were in love with that savage, but all came to end, I am choice a better quality of life for my children and also for me, no more tears, no more anguish of abuse provoked by Esteban.

Until there was a day when the authorities took pity on us, but for it to happen this we had to go through a lot years extremes of violence domestic.

Meanwhile you could see very happy to my daughter Peggy, telling me Mother, **I'm seeing our depart DAY**, to begin a new life in the capital, yes responding my mother one more day sweeter.

The day arrives, but we are full filling sad because my littler sitters state with my grandma, better to save my mother life.

Finally we got to Aunt Felicita house, I felt weird, she scared, and the communication with aunt Felicita is poor, because we have little communication.

Chapter # 23

TRAVELING ARROUND THE BLUE SKY

Only lived a dream flying in the blue sky.

Just a dream many times can give relief in moments difficult to so much sadness that was living, so much uncontrolled violence at home against my mother.

Didn't know what a joy of playing with others girls, wake up early so go to school and talk with my classmates, well no, at school my mind or thoughts in my house with Mom., but my body in the school and my main to think in what would happen when Dad, arrives home ad the worse is not me at home to defend her.

I ignored in the school to my classmates because I am living a sad life with my parents. but they don't known what I am living a world different from all classmates, they also made me bullying, probably they did not know the sad life then I been lived at home.

After a life confuse; in my home a nice dream what made me happy it happened for only few moments and remember it forever.

I explained how starting this dream:

The <u>dream begins in the threshold </u>of the door of my house. Already almost getting dark, had in that time of my dream I had about six years old, I was exactly standing in front of the door of the entrance of my home., being over there could observe to the right side came in my direction a beautiful lady, hair golden, about thirty years old, appearance with elegant dress, tall brought dress very blue sky with a background white around the neck and long sleeves with a big ribbon look long cloth white that crossed lowered the waist, she came up to me front me, said want give a walk? I answered yes, didn't know her, didn't know who was she and so easily answered yes, I remember that when went with her, did not think In my mother, nor the rest of the family, She, take my hand and we walk then I saw by myself sitting in a fanny fishing boat Kayak, similar to the ones people use for fishing in the sea, but here flew like a plane that in those time neither know.

with the violence we lived not to think in planes. never hear something about airplanes my mother did not have time for talk to us, she had to have the careful by our diary live and expect a husband, drunk abuser.

Yes only remember when she took my hand, and when saw is me flying with Mss. Darling, we sit in a small fishing boat, together see the front and around a beautiful splendor never seen before.

both sitting in the middle of the little boat or kayak plane, we flew like a plane around the sky blue it going so fast because my hair looked well extended, that already my hair, it was long and wavy, I can see by myself how fly in the beautiful universe, BLUE SKY.

everything looked _ marvelous we were flying around the sky blue it was so difficult to describe what I was looking at the sky shining blue _ by its stars, so precious everything that was seeing that I did not dare to ask Her anything, didn't have fear was happy At that moment that I was with her, my family did not exist, my mind was in white was only amazed at what he was looking at .the blue sky panorama look beautiful seeing the shining stars _ wonderful giving a light that made make the earth shine so beautiful and Inexplicable that light wonderful that it made me feel happy .

Today that I have traveled on a plane is completely different from my dream, this journey was Wonderful very Majestic my hair look fly, nice fresh the air on my face, since we travel without any outdoor protection is something that has never existed,

but my dream traveling around from heaven blue It was something wonderful, I can't compare to traveling on a plane at night and fly over las Vegas, nothing comparable what I was living with the lady in blue and white .during my wonder trip smiling and observing all around me She asking me did you like the trip? In fact responding, yes I did..

Very happy traveling with Mss. Darling blue and white.

My family did not exist until she told me; we have to go back, we walking with and, soon we arrived to my home.

This dream helped brighten my life, help me feel happy helped giving an escape to my life, Now I think that it dream was a escape from the terrible reality of domestic abuse that we lived at home, whenever I remember saw in that little kayak.

That dream has been Unforgettable, it felt so real. There are times that I think How real I lived that dream, in that moment she was my angel, made me happy moments, created the situation of a dream.

A dream what made me happy.

Memory of the dream, when She hold my hands, and we went by the same place where she appeared, but I don't remember the place where we take the kayak, only same place way when we went a back home, she left me in front door.

Chapter # 24

TWELVE YEAR OLD "PEGGY"

My mother finally separated from my father, we are living in Managua with aunt Felicita house.

we have moved to the capital, the challenge economic us was hitting, the family support did not exist, we were adapting to another way of living in a life of terrible poverty, many sometimes we had nothing to eat.

When us we moved to the capital and my mother had three pregnant months.

My aunt's husband, Armando, worked as a Butler in the Santa Elena Club, owned by Ex-President Somoza, always brought lots of club food that left over and they gave him. But they did not share with us they looked as strangers and ignored our hungry face, they set aside what they would eat and the rest they threw to the pigs that were creating in the back of the house, they did not share with us, either asked if want some but we only observed them. .

Here comes the life challenge mi Mom, working in a drying cleaning they pay so little not adjust to buy the basics first necessity food.,

In each pay she made sure to buy rice, beans, eggs, sugar, and oatmeal, but many times this did not arrive not one _ week, little by little went adjusting to the expenses and the way of eating. To adjust the week,

Went doing our own menu:

Breakfast:

Coffee with simple cookies, it was big.

Lunch:

Rice with beans

Juice, oats

Dinner:

The most times, water with sugar and simple biscuits.

My mother we said that should save, for have our own house, since we did not want still living with her sister.

My Mother have to make overtime working hard her stomach growing sad for her, because already came pregnant, we slept on the floor, it was not comfortable for her at night.

Months late another girl born her name Nancy; my Mom prepared for the childbirth and she save some money at least would not work for a month.,

The months years pass and finally the house was made pure sacrifice, in control all expense, save a lot food, clothes and shoes, the saving help and finally b already we had our house little big tree rooms living room, and kitchen, arrived the day we moved into our own humble home .

1. But our does not end here poverty, perhaps it is worse, more expenses, not yet _ adjustedmon's budget, for food.

One of many days we did not have sugar to sweeten our water, it was simply water with sugar, and one of my sisters went to see Aunt Felicitas asking for sugar, and they don't open the door.

there were all my cousins and my aunt, the window was open, and my sister prepared to enter through the window, like children without prejudice because it was the house of our Aunt, when my little sister was putting his hands to enter we could see my cousin

Marco, closing fast the window staying her hand pressed and leave over there pressed by some minutes, he could take out, with their hurt hands we returned home and without the sugar very sadly . We besieged that we did not have family.

The birth of the girl gave her luck, months later my mother found other better work, bought the prepared milk for my little sister already bought it by boxes, to avoid us the effort to prepare the milk for my little sister.

Before was so great poverty that we did not to buy sugar, this was the irony of life being daughters from a family of ranchers.

Many times I have thought in the destination when gives us many tests, maybe also we were the cause to measure the feelings of other people like my aunt and her family, they were not kind to us .

When one is poor and comes close to a relative, too can be a friend, they are embarrassed many times by our appearances; perhaps they think we are stealing his space.

my twelve years my school days continued dramatic, I did not change my posture, very quirky in silent with a face strong, my classmates did not like me, they gave me a bad nickname, called me GALLINA CULECA, they called me So because my hair was frizzy, and they said it was so fluffy as he body a culeca hen, I didn't really look at the comparison because my hair was beautiful, I didn't really bother me the name they had given me.

But I was trying to be strong and show him that I didn't mind. the bad nickname they gave me, and I'll show them that my hair is elegant and it's my style, so I ignored them .

Always at the end of the school day, a group of classmates would wait for me. in the street to make fun of me they called me with a bad name CULECA hen, the further aggressive of them snatched my backpack _ throwing to the ground, like a ball in position to hit it, and in fact they left kicking her down the street after crying trying to get my backpack, they did all days and would stop half a block before getting home and leave running.

Nobody defended me, the girls just laughed; I looked like a crazy trying to catch it. .

I didn't know as tell to my Mom, and Teacher what is happening to me with my classmates of class.

My companions did not stop harassing me, they sat behind me, pulled my hair, made the paper in the form of a ball and threw it at me, carelessly one of them scratched my homework with a big X, they were so cunning that even the teacher was didn't suspicious of everything they did to me.

I spent it in expectation of the surprise that they could give to do .

I do not deny that the bad name they gave me; did not have sense, my hair curly and well light blond with light brown. For me it looks nice,

I don't understand because they did not like me light honey eyes color, my skin white and my physiognomy look like a doll's, I think that this is the reason that my companions boys and girls have me envy, I am better than them .

Good for what to think I hope that comforts me, why? I do not anymore that I can do? I can't stall this situation; I am already frustrating, when got home, quietly without doing no noise neither comment about it. The bullying still by the student in the Capital school, I don't understanding why?

Tomorrow another day of class, I do not deny that it bothers me the bad over name gave by my companions from school, but I must learn to have further courage of which already I have, I will not allow them and with my parents nothing to do that stress to continue me offending since it mortifies me too much, I have to raise my self-esteem at least _ do he effort that what they tell me does not bother me and show them that I am the most pretty in class and I'm sure it will be my mechanism defensive .

I wonder maybe I can do so that they stop and understand that they are doing wrong?

My plan starts today Monday, with my week class. I arrived at school, and sat down in class, but my head had many thoughts, the issues at home, the harassment from my classmates and about All my bad score that I couldn't get up. I needed help and the worst thing that happens to me is when the teacher asks me for the tasks, a just stay quiet. I have to do something, and the best way is to ask the teacher for help t but I am filing shame, I'm a bad student, because I don't have on time my homework, my Mom not have time to help, well a way will find, but this can't continue I don't know either as improve what is happening.

Chapter # 25

THE GIFT OF MY FIFTEEN BIRTHDAYS

Tula, commandment her filing in that time what can I say about my fifteen years, maybe I can say a lot or not too much, it was to this age when the love that came feeling because of my mother _ crumbling .

Why began to die the love for my mother?., that beautiful love that I had for her; it's was exactly the sixth day of June one thousand nine hundred seventy three. My Mom forced me to get married with a man I didn't love, I think my mother didn't really love me such as me to her, maybe _ was acting for their own interests, it would be his ambition that was wearing by wrong away; maybe _She think it's the best for me? Just only she can answer the question.

I am thinking that really my mother it is getting mentally sick, it has changed his character dramatically, his bad temper begins to worry me, she when to registered in a school religious with schedule should be from six in the morning to five in the afternoon, late asking she why she decide that school, I have get up early, Mom, that school it is so far like twelve miles from home.

She told me it's because I didn't want to see you at home. I state quit for some minute because I couldn't understand she but she still said that I am the most very disobedient, but don't like that school. then, she hit me for no reason, left me big bruises.

Any way I went happy to the school I liked school, but bothered me some time when I asked for mom for the money to pay the school transport, simply said today you not go to class, your compartment bothered me mother why you didn't me before? Why? I had get up very early dress and when I ready to leave you mom easy tell me you not go to class, it caused me sadness, now my main changed since now preferred go to class than stay at home I couldn't stand for my mom bad attitude _

The aggressive way of my mother I was already depressing to the point that there was I lost the will to live, I just wanted to die, the opposite when we lived with dad, I wanted to Live to take care of her . but now I feel that I am dying, my mother 's attitude hurts me a lot .

One of the many days in walking to school an adult young man of about ten years older than me, he sat next to me, When sitting down very friendly and talkative also he did many questions, told me that is a Engineer agronomist student, he looked very young shorter than me, very nice, we talking until each one arrived to our destiny, but it was not last time, continually found him in the bus stop, until one day he wonder for my address and if could visit me, I told him, with emotionally, when you like.

He looked good young man student in his last year of engineering degree _ Agronomist, he starting to visiting me, almost daily, but I considered it as a friend, nothing on my mind to be a boyfriends, but here coming a problem since my mother watching the continue visit from my friend, less pass many months then she telling me that I will be considering him like a future MAR RIAGE for you, I told her No Mom he's just a friend, Mom, I don't have any idea to get matrimony I am very girl.

Here the situation changes, my friend Manuel began to play game mom, I think he was noticing her intentions, and he began to behave very nice with her, it was la opportunity so that she would make me the game thought would convince me to accept him as my boyfriend.

he turned _ rude to me, in Sometimes he pull my hair, because

I didn't attention him, and told me So I very mad because you not like as you boyfriend. I notice that me indifference bothered him, but as already he had great confidence with mom, he didn't even bother in what she could say and it's obvious he wouldn't bother.

MAMA's pressure reached so much, that we are engaged; but it was not my intentions, simply was an objective of my mother, but my own object in the futures years fall in love with a person where I did not feel in a relationship forced such Mom doing now.

My mother doesn't understand my intentions; she breaks my feelings to the point of planning my wedding without my consent. I have not even turned fifteen years old. _

I ask my MOTHER, how I can marry with someone then I do not love? _ I feel so upset, but I swear I don't 'will spend a month with him; my mon answering categorically any way you will not leave he, because when a woman marries, she is obligate to take care of his husband, then I answered she, I'm sorry but you in wrong, mom, would you understanding that It can be happen when both love each other and that is not ours case; therefore I will marry to do happy him and you, and that it.

Several months by June 1973 were contracting marriage and my fifteen years would in November 1973.

since we compromised It was stressful to the point that one evening before the wedding we had a discussion in as for the wedding expenses; _ and my anger was so bad that I threw my wedding rings, but my mother insisted _ _ in fix the fight that she he left running to convince him to come back, and he could get . the wedding was planned, the place was chosen by my fiancé and it would be in the city of their parents, and they had to hire a bus to move the guests whatever for both family, but what happened?

the family wrote me a letter saying that they will not be at the wedding since I _ would be a hindrance to him and a retracted unsociable and would not be the wife indicated since I eat Engineer I would have to get along with their friends, so many rude words that it hurt the soul, I felt that I did not deserve that way of treating me, really that would be the biggest reason not to contract marriage. but for my MOTHER, nothing happen, and with my fiancé, in looking for a wedding event house was planned . quickly no time to wait, and my mon have to .hurried to founding a place for the event, impossibly we couldn't find a place and the best thing was to talk to the one who would be the godmother of the wedding who was the Owner of a Commerce Academy, like I said there was no time to wait and it had to be repaired he wedding venue And I asked if he helped me with the place and if it was possible make the wedding meeting _ at school, she _ very gentle she accept and the wedding go up all in favor of my mother

Arrive the wedding day June six of one thousand nine hundred seventy - three, my mother sent the bridesmaids to the beauty salon, she said you state here, and with respect to my such It seemed that it would not be my wedding that day, everything was almost normal there were two hours left for the wedding, and without know what do the worse than my mother left home saying I going for the cake, and she left me at home half hour later to my wedding soon appear my uncle Abel father brother, stay looking and looking me for some minutes and told me you will be in the church, is very late and you here . I told him that my mom left here in waiting for her, he wonders in asking for my wedding dress. I have it with me, he said very well said my uncle, and take the dress, shoes jars, rings, and we hurry. I remember that I left wear my pajamas and slippers, in On the way I asked my uncle to go with my bridesmaid house, when arrived there many friends were scared saying what happened to you we are expecting and thought that already you came from the church already married. I didn't tell them They have to help me and five of my friends went with me to room and began to help me get dressed makeup and doing my hair, I remember that it was not so difficult for them in make beautiful face but I would not stop crying they trying to make me fancy day and finally I am ready and we went to church, on the way still crying .

We arrive to the church finally ready for the wedding, when we arrived all guests my fiancé, the priest, expecting outside the church, it is over late two hours, my fiancé and the priest, was very angry, the priest told me many things that words took away by the wind I did not put attention, I was in complete stress, did not stop to crying.

well after the scolding, we went in, I wouldn't stop to crying felt like I was fainting to the point that priest stopped the wedding until I feeling better, when I felt better the priest wonder Yeah wished that he to be continue the marriage, I said yes, at the end of the wedding, my fiancé kissed me, and asking me, why you had cried I can see on the veil, gave me grief Because of him, I didn't answer anything . yes only thought he really loved me, but me don't, it make me fell pity for him, I know he's a great man. Sad for him may be one day will be love.

After the people got _ lined up on both sides so that when walked in that row the guests congratulate me, but I felt so bad when they congratulated me, further I wanted again to cry want to tell them stop congratulating me, I wanted go out running from the church, I felt like someone rescued me, I am filing sad. I have pain in my soul because my MOM, was not there, therefore it was not seeing my pain But I think that was his punishment she didn't see me in my wedding; after the cake she went home and did not arrive at the church, where we were Doing the meeting, I dove in a feeling of melancholy and really wanted to disappear from the planet

Neither of my parents were at the wedding, my uncle made of my father, and my mother who tied he marriage did not arrive Were many gifts from my classmates, friends of my godmother, some, relatives, but really the gifts did not interest me I don't know where were left I don't even remember to have open some .

fifteen days later come home to pick up some of my belongings, there my MOM was there, when she approached me I told her I didn't want to see her by a lot time, felt contempt anger did not want to know anything about her .

we left far from the city to a rice paddy farm property of President Somoza, there I turned fifteen years old and my gift was he pregnancy with my first baby, I do not deny that when I found out that I was pregnant, I felt happy dreamed of my future baby,

Past several months since I left, and I did not want see my MOTHER, since kept grudge .

seven months later came back, it was an unexpected day for her, and the meeting took place, the first thing she said; I'm sorry daughter, I really left by the cake; but my plans changed and my intention was that you no longer you will marry

Really MOM, I will never understand her, and if my Uncle had not arrived by me I was not married.

mother I thought that when you returned from buying the cake would feel bad for have missed the wedding,but reality I fell his love for me, but you right now would feel you conscience mortified. Or maybe you filling happy to have me married with you guy preferred; now all this done, now don't worry for me everything its fine. I know that you are happy.

Chapter # 26

ADULT "PEGGY"

Still Peggy in described part of her life; reflects on living with Tula and Esteban who are her parents.

Domestic violence causes countless disorders and confusion, but you have to be aware in mind the way to be or try to be happy, always tried to understand my mother even forgave her bad behavior because of how difficult it was been his life. About my father, important thing is to try to love by myself .for to be able love and understand to the people.

The path way are very difficult when had lived in domestic violence; it caused sad and depressed.

Domestic violence has been the worst experience that I have lived in my home, come in several stages since my childhood, teenager young girl until adult.

One year after the divorce from my parents the violence continued, this changed now my Mom against me, she take my dad place,. Differently _ but it was abuse, very rude punishments, the tenderness disappeared.

Before my parents' divorce I swore to by myself ever let any abuse from my eyes, ayes, but her everything forgave him by the abuse she suffered from my father.

I have learned to face the different difficulties of my life learning to live, and trying to be completely different from life in which developed, swore to make my life very different to my mom. Love my children and demonstrated respect for everyone, taking all the challenges with courage and dignity, and not fade by all the drawbacks in the course of life.

Now that I'm an adult, I visualize how beautiful life is, you just have to make an effort to cope with it, now I am proud from my children they take the goals necessary in try to been good citizen.

And I have taught them of the goals necessary to be good people.

I am forget and no longer thought in those sad things; appreciate today the life that God has given me.

My respect for Tula mon, a woman humble with her life of so much pain she did everything possible to take care of her children so that they did no lack anything.

All those suffering happened when lived in the Town of SAN FELIPE, where I'm sure they not forgotten TULA and ESTEBAN **THE WRONG LOVE STORIES.** I lived over there many years. So sad Enough reason that made me love much to my Tula MOTHER.

Regarding my mother had changed his mood very drastic, and we did not know really why her attitude changed, to a women very cold and rude with me.

2ND *edition*

TULA'S LIES

Contents

Dedicated

I dedicate this second edition with all my heart once again give a big hug to the people residents in all nursing home. Also all employees what make it work with love them.

Introduction

Want to clarify that the first and second edition have been used Names imaginary but just clarify that the first edition is attached to the second edition. First and 2nd edition are written as fiction story.Two stories in the same book; with the objective to following dram story*****

First edition: Please Dad don't kick my Mom.

The 2nd edition: Tula lies.

felt shame for the **DOMESTIC VIOLENCE from my dad toward my MOn, Since days** after My parents got married and me in my mother womb and my hard birth know for all town and family until the age of eight years, that situation did not stop until my mother abandoned him; a drunken, abusive father who didn't take pity on his children a lot less his wife. Then Peggy growing working hard with her mon for a better life, now the 2nd edition continue with Peggy and Tula, where Tula changed the her behavior as a lady rude and liar.

The second editing with details deeper and sadder to learn that Tula has started with Alzheimer and dementia disease,

Family feel worried for her. Me Peggy, I took almost six year trying to know how it disease works in the human with healthy and by behavior of conduct, bad and good mood.

I have reasons why I think she not has that illness, but I am not the person who dismissed the doctor's opinions; I believe in them

I need be able to convince by myself to know if she is lies .

Tula, confused me and we accepted it as such, she was further beyond the unexpected, creating a disease where we should accept it, and all her insults and extortions trying to understand and believe that she has dementia and Alzheimer.

Hard for me to understand and make control her ended annoying and very angry with her, when a trying to calm his hallucination of rich lady. And we must be listen he; if we not, his character would be aggressive.

I am sure to study that disease. When, and where I don't know?

Theme # I

THE CHANGED GIVEN FOR "TULA."

From girl, when already had use of reason, I begged my mother let's go far away from my father, but she did not;

Now, really just my mother knew why she not leaves him

finally when reach my eight years old, my mother separates from my father, my life change really it would be for better or for worse, well our lives changed with more poverty, but with a little peace, we had moved to the capital, my mother came pregnant, now you can Imagine the gloom we went through .

We're passing the years, my mother in her main many plan for as; when me arrive to fifteen year old the best for her what me

Peggy, go get matrimony but some circumstance will be some time for good; it is why any person doesn't know what will be happen on that way. Here coming a changed;

My mother enter in a new relationship failed with a soldier, in that time she look for the opportunity what Peggy get matrimony she working in this chance with the recent graduate Engineer, it was too controversial but the marriage was consumed, then I moved so far from my Mon. and she still with the new failed relationship, procreating two children with great setbacks, one came out sick with lip cleft, she lost his work one thousand nine hundred sixty nine (1969).

The soldier fall in war January Nineteen two thing happen with this soldier that day abandoned her; some people said what he was died.

She, don't no known anything about him, Since that day she change her mood, very mad, hard to understand or socialized with her, suffering in silence.

since she was in charge of the laundry of the military mechanic school, therefore for work in the guard, and a soldier's wife, it deprived to Tula, express their feelings. She was a close to fall in jail _ for his ties of his work. She suffered the lost of father of his children, it sad situation forced to Peggy helps her, in everything she need.

Peggy said I love mon so much; but my mother began to take advantage and each once asked me more and more money until gave her two payments mortgage from my home, until here because my husband require those money, I had to said what that gave to my mom.

Since that day stop me to do that.

very upset with my husband; of course this situation with my mom made me take care of my matrimony, but what else could to do meanwhile, well I was growing as a women adult, since she forced me to get marry before turning fifteen. I need take my own decision.

I do not deny that my mother 's presence made me feel good, she managed my marriage, even my thoughts, I do not deny that while I have been merry and had all necessary for my home, since my husband is an Engineer Agronomist who worked for big great farmer company. Poor Tula many difficult situation in her life was not careful and lost control of her actions.

But me Peggy I need take care for my matrimony.

Theme # II

BREAKS UP PEGGY MATRIMONY

Tula made a big mistake June 19802, seven years After marriage I got in divorce in mutual okay, for that date I had already graduated from high school, and was in the University, and to life it would change for me, but I was hoping for the child support from my husband for my children, well what I had to do yes look for work .

forced to search I work it was not difficult, but before separating process a loan real estate, they gave it to me in the name of my ex-husband, since I did not have credit because I did any work, now I have to ask to my husband to sign documents home loan.

But here came my big error, was when I separated the first thing what I did was accommodate my mother with all my siblings my mother and my two children we were ten in family, really I never imagined that the burden would be very big for me _

Now I need get a job it was no difficult for me, founding like in a Service company like as Assistant to the director, great for me they paid good salary more the child support coming from my ex-husband Timo. Until now working fine. at home the boss was Tula mother, she did not work but two of my brothers Yeah they worked, my mother collected the money for each brother and siblings, but she don't make any plan to pay the home bills it should be fair _ _ Of course it didn't suit her while with my salary and my children's pension I paid all the household expenses, food and utilities . Little by little I left narrowing economically until what I did not have enough to buy clothes a lot less to give me a recreation with my children to go out to eat at the restaurant something cheap not nothing, I went out Complete with my income . Not even to buy a lunch at work, sometimes I would go without eating anything, until I got to chance, but my brothers Yeah you had to enjoy and buy what they liked, even go eat out. The ideology mom it is you are the owner home you need paid every expense at home, siblings, they living free my home.

Many year pass and my brother got drunk many times after work, every day I felt submerged in the whims of my mother, disrespect toward me, with verbal fights daily and EVEN MORE SO WHEN SHE DIDN'T HAVE MONEY, this caused a characteristic and to calm down Her, yes to give money even though I need paid all the household expenses except the phone bill it

Is own paid by my brother. To make her happy and stop her bad mood with many rude ugly words, I have to ask for my next advance payment at work I make it only for give my children peace at home.

For love to my mon, I am make complicated and difficult my life. started suffocate without knowing when this nightmare would end.

But the verbal fights also can't stand her blackmail, and now having to argue with my drunken brother.

Impossible to stop this situation, to this point I am deciding to move with my children in living with my best friend Teresa.

without waiting further I called by phone talking with Teresa, about my situation an atmosphere suffocate at home she friendly said when you want move here you are welcome. Minute late packed our children and me clothes and left with my two children, notice my mom very relaxing sit in the living room watching a television.

Away from home it made me uncomfortable we missed ours

beds but it is better what returning home. After a week we missed our space.

Some time I talking with Teresa concerning children saying they don't have to be going worries also should work for a plan to improve the situation ; but I really don't have no ideas how improve the situation between my mother and me, end the conversation between Teresa and me,

We concluded to return to my house sooner I can. In the next day It would be seven in the morning is

When got back home I found my mom could without comment jus like showing a home of peace. She felt like the owner of the house. days after arrive home she still discussed for nothing.

Many times we have to take decisions although us it hurts, I forgave her all offenses, thinking always in the treatment that my father gave her.

Past seven years that I trying to understand mom it seems that history repeats itself, exactly Years than my mother stood the abuse from my father; and she continued a history more against us .

One day returning from my work, she with her same attitude I reached the point that I grabbed courage and I told her that had one day to go out my home with your two children, and each two week come back for money so that your maintenance, and I want it to be clear: tomorrow when come back from work, I hope you and your Children far away from my home, is time to have little peace for all in this home. I need my space. Goodbye Tula, I'm ashamed to tell you Mom, I fell what my soul hurts but what I am doing is the right thing. I know what one day this pain will disappear because you are my mother.

For now better if you go out from my life for some time?

Early the next day I went to work without comment, thinking in the decision taken and doubt in what if she would really leave, pass the day, and on my return home to my surprise it had gone with my two means brothers, staying in my house my three brothers, Alexandrina,, Esperanza, and Daniel.

could not believe she gone. His home is located in a city about sixty miles from the Capital, with pain in my soul but she had to leave, my brother Daniel, felt sad, me also, it was necessary, we passed seven difficult years to get to take bliss decision, but I love her a lot and always accepted her his whims but now she go far and we can't understanding her.

but already was in I play the tranquility of my children and mine too .

As the days go by and we get home we all feel his absence, the house was felt in silence could _ feel that something was happened there, with her was a situation toxic, and manipulated, all happen when she packet out of money.

A month ago t, and my mon, adapting to her own home, I told her to come every couple week for money, but no, she come every Saturdays at an early morning she in our home in asking money, and we gave her everything she need. Then she left happy, we were controlling the situation regarding their abuses. _

Months after MAMA, she left from our home; begin to emerge problems with my brother Daniel, he was getting back alcoholic after work, irresponsible had assigned the responsibility to pay the telephone services, and it no longer paying on time . His salary did not adjust, because he took it in liquor, the only obligation that he did not forget share some money for "mon" and the rest money was taken in liquor, began to annoy I had to said Daniel that have to leave my house, and responding category saying no Peggy,. and been here for I don't know how long time been in you home, that fine I will try to find a husband, am sure what you will be going out this home because, you are irresponsible with you own obligation.

It's been a year since mon, left my house, while since long trying to manage us to her craving, every weekend at early morning comes home with his own sermons; wonder when my mother will understand, that I am very repentant he have them left enter my house, but now it's really not like do it understand that she must drive to his own home and what we deserve respect, and how make to understand that now not accepted from her, no more abuse.

The love that I had by she is _ breaking.

do not lose hope of finding a good man to marry me, but I follow praying, that one day will happen I know if having a husband all It will change and I hope for the better.

the weather it happens, and the fights on weekends _ siblings and me don't stop with my mother for money, my brother has graduated as a public account, he has a good work and salary, but it is getting back alcoholic like my FATHER.

I'm very repentant in got divorced,

sacrifice my marriage to house them all out of love for them to have a life better ; but I'm the one who's been harmed, yeah we have past more than seven years together with my brothers and now what else I long to get married so that my mother and brothers respect me .

Now my mother has started a new drama, when she doesn't have money she becomes crazy, she starts talking to herself, she thinks she's a women very important, adapt the posture of a women millionaire, what someone sending messages on radio and television, when we try to calm her down she gets upset to the point that she turns aggressive, sometimes she plays sick _ how is it missing he air to breathe and faints, that us does feel us very bad.

I've gotten to the point where I feel like my life is hell at home to the point that really I want disappear with my children from my family an living in a place so far from brother and sister then my mother, made my life miserable.

have passed eight years Since I got divorced, my mother moved back to her hometown, but we have not seen any change, rather more _ expenses, one of my sisters, Alexandrina, went to the United States " with so little money, only with an acquaintance of the cast who always brought people helping them ""to enter the United States illegally, by then, I were liquidated a small business, and I could only give two hundred dollars, but for that time the relations with my sister were not very good but try to contribute in some few dollars, really what was within my reach .

In this subject I could give tells that history has repeated itself in a very _ strong, since my mother, passed exactly seven years married subjected to abuses by my alcoholic father. Years further late, for circumstance of life, my mother came to live with me and they were seven and over almost eight years abusing me asking for money.

When my sister move to the United States of America, my mother I was in charge of my niece and my sister had started sending _ Dollars some TWO HUNDRED dollars by month. But the bad habit of Mama still in asking money now she said for makes repair her home.

Tula, don't have any appreciation for any one.

Theme # III

PEGGY- RE-MARRIAGE

My desire to find a special friend, or my future husband and him will be found me in my home, I am crazy lady? But at the same time I saw it as an impossible dream, but its my wish.

One day appeared a man on the bus stop when I going work, it happen most of the time in the same time, nothing in my main, only observe him because he's look handsome, and sometime we talking about our job and house address then the bus arrive we go ahead on our way.

One unexpected day this guy appear in from my door it was surprised for me, He look upset after hi wherever, he said I need make a phone call I had an emergency; sure coming, and use the phone.

That day we were little conversation, since that day him came to visiting me for a long three months for my surprise he asking for matrimony surprise for me I did not expect short time for such a great offer.

I do not deny what I expected and the offer arrives at my home, my prayers were heard,

After he left me with a great news, I am very happy, saying: finally found a young man who offered me marriage, it further funny it was that he asked me got married and he's tell me same month and day, when I was marriage; was scared for me because he did not know anything about the dates of my previous marriage, It just was coincidence, and I told him woo, really fast we going change for that day we set the matrimony date. it was May Twenty Three nineteen hundred seventy seven. Month and day to my previous matrimony was changed.

The day arrives and we were in matrimony. June 23 1977.

One year after my re-marriage, two siblings live in my house, my MOTHER, still asks her quota, now I'm married, also I was talking with one those my brother alcoholic telling I hope that the situations at home change comes true such as I told you that everything switch when I get married, well now everyone is _ carry very good, except my mother nothing changed to align her.

The relationship with my sister in the United States has improved, to the point that asked me to visit her.

Pass the months and four months after being married; apply in my work a six-month leave to take a break that would allow me visit my sister in the United States.

In our home now there is peace, my new marriage very good, it was worth it the one that my mother left home, for the good of all and I think that for her too.

six years after getting married, I prepared my vacations to travel to the United States. My sister sent me the gift of ticket to visit her. _

Felipa the babysitter in charge of the house and the take care of my two children until my return.

When I arrived in the United States, my sister clemencia, had plans for me, but I did not intend to stay with her, since my children and my husband were in my country,

therefore I should return, my intentions simply vacation .

I stayed with Clemencia, for five months

I worked as babysitter to save for my ticket and buy some gifts to my family. Were five months, those month were so sat and crying?

Every weekend verbal fights with my sister because I wouldn't stay to live with her, but it was more strong love my children and should come back and make plans for the future.

Upon my return from the United States, I was surprised, I no longer had work, they had me removed from my position as advises business without any excuse, they had me made a transfer to other institution with a verbal transfer

to another Institution Followed with the dismissal letter. The transfer did not make me logical, since while _ was in the United States the calls were constant that I will return, and on my return over there I had my salary accumulated by five months for it seemed true to me Fantastic, I didn't even expect it and accept my dismissal.

Analyzing the problem in my job, token with my ex-husband to see the possibility of obtaining visa for my children and bring them to the United States, without any obsession did the paperwork, everything it was very fast in a month were ready the documents to travel to the United States, leaving at home, Alexandrina sister Daniel and my husband .

I'm seeing what necessary leave the country is, however I know that my husband will join us since he _ has ready his visa

Now my life switch since I will dedicate myself to my true family my two children and my husband, I hope a better life out my mon, and siblings.

Theme # IV

LIVING IN IN MY DREAM "PEGGY"

When you are a professional in you country of origin and _ move to the United States of North America, quickly could visualize that nothing at all is easy to live without any support, you need a strong hand around you.

When got a refugee our life changed most of the time for good; some time want to come back to own country because feel hard search a dream but it's over; it hitting very strong because in this country I can't not walk without a stick to hold me.

Any job is welcome for me and when arrive to this country the profession is not working here is patience to learning the transition in that stage we need food, clothes, lodging it no coming free, It to work and working hard. it make me proud with dignity to build my dreams. It was no easy in the Unite state, I need working hard. Because work hard is building a great dream.

.
.

MY STAY IN THE UNITED STATES.
Just one month after I moved to live in the United States of

North America, I am feeling Like a bird without wings, feel like need support to get out go ahead, my sister is not enough, need to have my husband to support each other, because only then could go out forward . Here I have realized that only a husband responsible could be the strong bar for together go out forward.

Now I'm watching the only possibility for my husband to come to the United States as soon as possible is to buy him a travel tiket, and who could _ do? I don't have work here only my sister, for that I have to see the way she accept and talking with his husband since he is the one who has the money to be able buy he travel ticket to my husband then we will pay.

the emotion of his arrival to the airport of the Angeles, comforted me, because I was sure what when his coming our economic state will be change for better; that day seemed so long to me since arrived at around eleven at night, I felt a hope in my life .

A few days later, my aunt Chana help in prepare document for immigration forms two week after coming to united State, my aunt husband Cristobal founding to my husband a job.

Now living in the United States of North America I have learned to walk and a little to run, I have learned that this is the country of opportunities, without discriminating.

Worth so much effort to see my true dream made reality? Without a doubt, it has been worth.

My life has been one of defiance and injustices always are in way.

I have not stopped to date to say I already did it, many times I thought that already there was reached my American dream, but no, I've had many American dreams . The American dream is not just having a house, a car, it's not that for me, it's how I feel in all the aspects.

Keep going, and keep going, I don't stop until I reach my American dream, I realized that if you arrive with a lot effort in the end can say yes I can, but I give note that haven't reached, I feel that I need work more .

You will see part of what I mentioned sacrifice and injustice, end the cycle from Tula, my mother.

Nineteen Hundred eighty eight, it's when most of my family

moves to the United States, my husband and me, we were able to rent an townhouse with three bedroom in the City Chino California.

Three months after having arrived in this country I began to study English, and fits mention that the little I studied English in our country, it was useful, and still in the University of the Utah.

the change of the language hitting us hard Spanish to English, since we started learning to speak as the children, with words and phrases, relating them to our diary live .

Move to living In the United States, for me is necessary try to adapting a new customs of life, process as learn to crawl later walk and known many forms or customs and the most import, the barrier to learning English with words and phrases, and talking such as when begin to development, reading, writing, and speaking, the daily language, but no only english I was starting since cero because is complete different culture. And why said barrier because it's in spend time, money, location and transportation. And I had those until having wings to fly for do this entails a process of knowledge and time. For everything learn in this country was a new step in my life. Every work was a skill of knolled for me was necessary adapting as much possible, therefore it was my priority adaptation.

The profession and experiences that I brought from my country help me a little by little to visualize and get better _ analyze to adapting my knowledge to other similar here it help me to make more easily adapting to work and study.

How much I thank my husband who allowed me study and support me in everything necessary, but do not believe my life has not been so easy I have struggled against the current with my family, coworkers, but my determination has always been do things the best of my ability _ work, study and taking care for family at home, very hard but I did.

Every day try to do the best.

My American Dream have no yet now, I need work little more, building with rock, over rock so my work will not fall easily,

Until that happen it's when I can said finally I have my America Dream, by November, twenty nine, one thousand nine hundred eighty nine 1989.

I gave birth to my third son here in the United States, I named him, will they ask me because Liberty peace?, because simply, we come to live in a free country;

my son is the product of our Freedom, and freedom for me it's courage, Effort, dignity and peace. It is beautiful living in this country United States of North America.

I'm thankful to this Country that adopted to sime family and me.

We are blessed and for me and family really it is our Dream Americano.

As mentioned previously, working hard until tiredness, my husband with up to three jobs, has work is his happiness.

THOUSAND NINE HUNDRED AND NINETY.

For that date I had already certified and obtained my professional license, but that wasn't for living, just a little help in our economic at home made it for seven years living in New York.

NINETEEN NINETY -FOUR

Life _ economy was not good only one temporary jobs a week very difficult, and we take the decision move to other state. I felt sad because the only thing I thought crawling again. Move to other state neither family, nothing but it was not so, I found some people who knew me and had been working with them, that make me comfortable more save in a new estate.

FEBRUARY TWENTY THREE, ONE THOUNSAND NINE HUNDRED and NINETY FOUR,

That year my second child bore here in North America, New York, being this my penultimate of four children.

My husband continues to work hard with two jobs.

Two months after had my newly born I started working in the same company that my husband works full time. Up to this point our stability economic us toward feel good, well our issues economic are staying back, already we are living with little stress economical. work permits they renewed it for us each year and it was very well because before we started with three months, six months, and now better each year, and our immigration case in California we had to be traveling sixteen hour to re new our authorization work, everything for have a job.to make our life Happy.

Theme # V

WITH TEARS OF COURAGE "PEGGY"

August,16, one thousand nine hundred ninety seven, 8/16/1997, I fell In this world nothing has been to me easy, everything has cost me a lot effort, many setbacks with my mother, in my work and what has led me to prevail is the good sense that I have handled my situations some have _ broken my heart, to the point of thinking because with me, but in this life he engine of my life they have been my children ; they gave me and give me the strength to continue trying hard

We had stable work, too our little tax preparation business _ working fine, you can say we are stabilizing our economic life, my eldest son ready go to a mission.

My motto is that one time _ you feel very well financially you think that everything always the same way, I was forgetting that in life has setbacks, yes, now I have a good moments, but what happen when thinking for something bad come ugly, to my main coming ideas no good, like now what happen if loss my job.?

No, why I am thinking in situation no good.

I thought that everything going fine, I was completely unaware that I had no status migratory defined; Here the unexpected happens to me, in waiting for an political asylum approve; ten year after living in the Unite State I received my deportation letter with the Judge appointment to look at the final decision.

When I got that letter I felt like a bird with the clipped wings, I am upset because all my illusion is going to the ground.

Two month ago bought a new house; when I did it everything look very well; my husband and me working in the same company of manufactured of products electronic. Here the ironies of life; Two days after that my son's departed for a mission from our religion; and my daughter in the Elementary School, now both children and me in the same Immigration processing

My other scary, no job, will be loss the house.

On my interview with the Judge, explained what my political asylum was no approve and I would no longer renew my work permit obvious what I left without a job. This decision also it affected my children they are in my application.

I see luck is no with me, events continue not for best; after a week also my nice left home when she's know my situation with Immigration. Many event make changed my diary living.

spend days trying to assimilate my new situation and one came on way, as my husband had in force his work status, it make sense good idea for a new business, without money, only with credit cards.

One of those days a new business comes to my mind; retail furniture _ taking advantage the place at the tax office, which for true it was big. Thought in the furniture store, and with less expenses only touched remodel it make space for new business Well, I have already my plan, now I have to talking about it with my husband; he will have the last word, because, he will have the last word since is only one who did not receive deportation .

Seeing the possibilities _ in which furniture store worked, I would have to analyze the furniture market. Here my plans one, them be contact some financing loan and furniture suppliers? without losing a lot time research furniture distributors _ _ located in California and contacted them, they requesting a license for furniture retail, without hesitating I started he business process and obtained the license and proceeded to request _ catalogs and wholesale prices, it was very ambitious since the _ furniture They came from a Middle Eastern country and were too much cheap and looked good _ price vary by style and quality all within the reach of the possibilities of the clients .

Still thinking, this business will be fantastic for making money! Because furniture like retail are cheap.

Finally the furniture store started working but _ _ here comes he effort from my husband have to work hard with two jobs, say three with the furniture store, also one those job, is by the night, that why he sleep few hours, I know it is so hard for him.

Most of the time he help me in furniture assembling; we still work like that in waiting for a new immigration law.

The Immigration Judge_ was kindly left me live permanent until an immigration law favored me and so process my residence and my two children, meanwhile I should not have worked in none company until obtain my permanent residence. here in the United States of North America.

Well I could say that we were very lucky since the _ asylum was not approved but we could stay in the country in waiting for a new immigration law staying a hope open; the most nice happening is that my husband had a job and current his asylum and work permit. _That meant other open-door to living here for our family.

My husband continued with his three jobs, did not complain and maintained a good cheer up knew it was striving a lot and he did it so for our children because he did not lack anything at home.

many times asked him how get energy for work lot twelve hours by night, answered me sarcastically nothing else yes drinking Coca-Cola.

The furniture business _ really was a illusion did not generate Income rather expenses, and every day felt that we drowned financially with the line credit little by little our credit cards going to the top credit.

my husband insisted in that we need closed the furniture store; but really, it scared me just thinking that I didn't have a job.

Now I am learning that the stubbornness can lead me to financial failure. Ignored the times that my husband advised to close the furniture business, really _ us this causing a stress economic we do not have Profits since instead of growing sales dropped every day, and we borrow more and more .

The furniture business _ was as open box without recipient, only the illusion of the prices it were very low, with the hope of gain good money but, it was allusion, and my big problem.

Many furniture is not easily changed or replacement often, some take years to replace,

Few people can afford to change it every six months.

I forgot that detail before install the furniture store.

Using logic, the best thing should be stay at home in waiting for my immigration documents. uncertain at that time. but the despair of not being able to pay my debts led me to the worst and without being able to close it.

Ironically could not seeing the exit towards the closing of the furniture store, the kept thinking that little by little sales would improve.

I am Filing like a selfish in pushing to my husband to work until the tiredness, but we don't has any alternative, yes was for look somthin better.

Two years has passed and my son comes Back from the mission with plans to get married.

Immigration law now was open the new program Nacara, was open and we get the residential green card residential and my son getting married too.

We continued working in the furniture store and my husband with his three jobs, still with the house it was refinancing.

but we no longer adjusted to pay the expenses, we refinanced the house but do that was a big obstacle by the future to sell it.

The refinancing happening the year two thousand five, therefore we have to wait.

Now we have our green car residents status it will going help to founding a better job.

though now our situation with the change of status things _ are much better.

To the point that the money from the previous house sale no long existed because it had spent, this entire economy thing looked bad to us took by surprise.

To this time already there was acquired my permanent residence all my family with the Nacara law, but now no longer had work we continued with our servicing office.

And finally we talking with my husband and take the decision to close the furniture store, for now we don't have time schedule.

Theme # VI

PEGGY'S TENDER AMBITION

Every day miss studying. I think that studying gives me the strength to be useful, and that is my tender ambition here in North America it is my need, my ambition, how to do it, will be my challenge.

Always looking to the future other time thinking what and who to do,

We decided together with my husband that I'll to register again in the Community college, also apply to scholarship for advanced English class as second language lacky I apply to scholarship, Well I did the entire study plan and started to study, finally got radiating by June six, 2006, I pass may class and get my 2nd professional license. then was move to the University, to study English class, because want to take the TOEFL practice test prep.

That day came very happy to my English class, was exactly six in the afternoon, when he teacher started and talking about that day

was June 6, 2006, I listening part of that confersation about that day, I got in nerves because that day I got my hard professional tes and was exactly that day. and at that time six in the evening, I been in English class and the teacher comment about that day, I was scared, because I was trying to pass the test many time until that day can do.?

coming to my main many idea, was no easy my graduate and was my obsession thinking to make money in the future.

was not so easy graduate agent very hard understand the terms, it require a good base of English, although already was studying in San Matheo Community College in California and in the still So needed more, but in the end I did it.

In my first year working in my new job my income rise to thirty six thousands.

Well that improve our situation economic and everything was going well.

JULY, TWO THOUSAND SIX.

We decided to sell our house since the prices had been increased; part of the profit would be used for the premium of a new house,

The search for the house began well, after we found nice house in the West City a nice place and of more value, quite, with big spacious rooms, and living room, nice home. Would this be my American Dream? However it remains to see.

The ambition is eating my brain, thinking what the opportunity arrive to made money in using the house as investment, need some update and my husband and me could be use some money that we have in saving when sold the old house. Well! the time is gold. to night have to talking with my husband about my plan.

The night arrive and my meeting starting

with my husband and show the plan to make more money, and the money we use in repair or update to the house, and the profit will be get if sold the investment home in one year.

When I showing the plan it look great for him and approved my plan, It's when I say by myself:

Peggy, what waiting? Is time do it.

"MAKE MONEY"

The improve starting

We remodel rooms, master rooms, kitchen replace carpet.

We use sherry wood furniture in design office room, finally finishing the remolding look nice. A month after the remolding home, coming the surprise special for me as Realtor full of illusion in Real estate business. "2008." the market coming down. Our house goes over price, cause it big Headache for me and husband starting hard, all saving we expend in the remolding home, surprise the Economic situation collapse.

I fell my heart so stress, All illusions turned into frustration; I was wrong again, I'm sorry for me husband, seeing the history repeats with different dram.

Two months before happen it, very happy my son went to the religion mission, I not idea how I couldn't tell him that I didn't have a job and we were losing our house, it seemed that it was walking on the same path full of thorns, it was hitting us hard, my youngest son began to misbehave in school. I felt like drowning in a glass of water. The good is what my husband didn't lose his job, but we couldn't afford our bills.

Finally, I send a letter to my son in the mission in explaining what we lose the house.

The ambition made me a trick, and without any hope, search aid in the unemployment office, what happen denied me for being sale employment.

I when apply in employment agency,

Looking for whatever work and they refer me a temporary work in the trash recycling, there will be work, but nothing there. The luck was cast.

To this time la recession hitting hard, there was no job availability, still in not lose the hope, and day to day still looking for job.

Theme # VII

TULA WITH ALZHEIMER

Now I knew about my MOTHER's disease, DEMENTIA AND ALZHEIMER? In Thousand Nine, my brother told me that was accompanied our Mom to the Dr., had made some tests to determine her disease of Alzheimer's, and Doctor, confirmed it. Me **Peggy accepted her, disease because the Doctor confirmed that she have Alzheimer disease and she back home with tidy medication and we need make the schedule for her to take the medicine.

they passed the months and her the same, I didn't look any changes of her disease, but my brother told me that she did not took the medicine, she collected and kept it, I asked her Why didn't take it ? She, just told me I don't want, her attitude made felt sat down to talk with her, I made her several questions about the interview with the Doctor, there I know that had told the same stories that many year ago I was hear from her. Were only imaginations created for her?

My MOTHER, towards things that only a person with his five senses the can to do, and it was what made me have doubt your _ disease, I tried to see the possibility of investigating his attitude, but could not find, if really She, had that disease .

BECAUSE THE DOUBT OF HIS ILLNESS.

At the end of this scene came to my memories all the inconsistency that my MOM did and said in the clinic with the Dr.

not convinced me his disease., I thinking she is lying to us making us believe that she is sick; that why she does not take the medicine, but I will look for a way to discover the truth.

I know her very well, the worst of all inconsistency or bad attitude happen when she needs some money.

Because I know her, simply when one of us, especially son or daughter who want to give money, it's when she start to turn on the radio and begin to talk as if they were on line like real conversation. On the conversation mentioned persons famous like artist, some time with the president, wherever, also many times adapting personality how if _ she is a millionaire women in use fraise and posture, making conversation with celebrities persons. Some time I tried to return her reality, impossibly couldn't get back at the end very angry and aggressive.

The queerest in her was that when she was traveling to his country of origin, she, purchased the plane ticket, prepared his own luggage and buying something that she would need for her trip. Doing it as an sensate person. She's change of attitude for her own interest. as a healthy person, traveling alone doing several scales in different Airports, and the worst did not speak English, and if she knew something but Tula is STUBBORN, and thinks what everyone around her forgives should speak Spanish.

I asked; Mother, what do you do when you traveling and don't like speak English? Well daughter, I just look around and realize if someone speak Spanish, and problem results. She still talking if I fell tired walking I make stop one of the cars what transport passengers in the Airport and they giving a ride until my station to take my airplane. After listening every step when she take a trip; all those make sense, like a healthy person.

Those answers and many more things she did, made me doubt her illness, Alzheimer and Dementia. Doctors diagnose her with that illness, for everything she did, but I live with her for about fifty five year with her living with all their inconsistencies, I am sure they would diagnose her with those illnesses. I have said what

I don't not want to be unfair to her, but I want to be very sure of her illness, I am MANY YEARS OLD F SEEING HER THE SAME DRAMA, AND SHE HEALS WITH MONEY. THAT MAKES HER HAPPY, AND ADORABLE.

Theme # VIII

HOPELESSNESS OF PEGGY

Trying to search for a job, to help a little financially at home and that we are losing our house for due payment, for consequence the recession what affected us we are for do something better, we are in de midyear two thousand ten, every day by the morning went out to look for a job with my friend Sara, along the way determined the place we always looked at EAST, Salt Lake City Utah, we really didn't know why that direction and every day we advance more at the East., one those days we saw a big and beautiful building color brown light, one on the right other on the left, I chose the left side because in the sing say Alzheimer, At that moment remembered my mother and her illness, but I don't have any idea what could happen when entered in the building with a little breath and very animated we entered, at the front desk, there a very elegant woman in a white dress what .look pretty.

She bring the prospect of working in the Alzheimer institution, but I have to wait for open usually will be end the month. But I need to certify as nurse Assist.

Started looking _ in the area of Alzheimer's and dementia

needed go to school acquire my certificate and they gave me ninety days to get my license. The opportunity to work here is true.

I saw a door open will soon work and could _ save at least the house where we living up to here there's my plan, now I'll see what comes by ahead .

when thinking in nurse home, especially in Alzheimer 's and dementia, from that point I not thinking in my situation economical, thinking in my mother, since in my mind _ I had the concern of having better knowledge about that diseases, but it made me impossible did not look as make it.

now I'm seeing that the door It opens for me and this is the opportunity to investigate further about that disease, there was no started my nursing assistant classes, but before that I started work in an Alzheimer's and dementia nurse home.

I'm being unfair in doubt my mother's illness maybe really she doesn't have those terrible diseases.

Here start my chance to meet what are the symptoms of Alzheimer's and dementia, and what else living with people with this terrible disease, but at this point there are two objectives very important work and have a salary and so on can help my husband do payments to the mortgage of the house where we are living, and the other dilemma is to finish or at least make sure she has really that disease, and take action necessary for the good of my MOTHER's health.

Without much thought, I made the decision go school to certify me as an assistant nurse, and when I began to study I began to relate in that medium, up to here all it's okay because I still did not imagine really as I would be work, I was going like pregnant women first timers very happy without imagining the labor pains that are terrible giving birth to have a child, like this I'm thinking very excited that I am giving the opportunity that before I looked at her unreachable now _ can say already did it without measuring none consequence ; Well, excited working there because will be knowing that my mother in reality had or no that disease

Here The unexpected is coming, in reality could not realize that work, never thought that I had many obstacles that would cut my wish for go to study for a nurse assist,

I had in my mind that could discover the disorders caused for that disease. Really forgot my panics and weaknesses; in those moments when I filling the application, just thought in my mon, for me it's the best opportunity to know the physical exhaustion caused by this disease.

My obstacles were very strong, therefore already _ I visualized that could not exercise the nurse assist.

Now they will ask me by what not? good here my answer : I have panic to the "DEATH" panic be alone in a room dark, panic seeing someone die, panic of touching a dead person, see blood causes me dizzy, see anyone vomit, including my

Children _when they were sick with vomited and bad smells. Therefore I must stop.

Seeing all the obstacles that I have really I am the least appointed to exercise that profession. but here this is my chance like I said previously, until now all this marching fine, everything this by wait ; I'll see what happens when finish the classes and come to do the practices .

"I don't have idea how control my soon arrived practice days here _ _ The difficult part was coming for me, only observing my instructor, but I didn't get into the work, I can't even imagine my expression at that time ?

The first day of practice, early in the morning, I could see some companions easily leaving could not exercise this job .

I remember that in my first day of my practices attend an incident in a bathroom, prying and walking to make that; but my training was the best in help to do my future work. Why my training help me?" because is a man, look strong, tall, of like fifty years old., and towards his work with a lot ability, while _ I felt like throwing up, I would not stop praying and, doing my training job, there was no special place saying my God, give me strength to be able in do this work, I do not deny that in my first training day this nursing assistant male contribute to start my new job, why he does being a man doing this work and why can't I do me ? Him, was the light in my way, I make a comment by myself He's my angel._

Only wished strength, to endure my trials, every day I was scared, and I did not stop praying and the prayers really strengthened me, because little by little I was learning the work and trying to do my best so all residents felt _ comfortable with me.

Doing the maximum effort to control my panic weaknesses,

DEATH, tried but wasn't really looking at me doing that job; but I still doing my training

But my fear followed latent.

When they had incidents strong that the legs or arms fractured, head, arriving and seeing the blood that terrible for me, but over there I was trying to help my classmates in the most can do, reaching towels, sheets or documents .

How to overcome my own obstacles, it seemed to me difficult; really in the interior of my soul it is hard for me, I do not deny that I want go out running and say no more . Every day the same phrase different panics, here doing this work, also my stomach upset, I am not prepared for such work, but I need this work and it is almost a fact, because it is the opportunity to have further knowledge about disease, Alzheimer and dementia.

This happened for him year TWO THOUSAND TEN, I finished my course as nurse assistant, also got my license with the Utah state.

My panics still, now I am certify and ready for get job.

I went apply in the area Alzheimer's and Dementia facility but need waiting until ends the month. because some are students and they leave, after that interview I insisted calling each week, me intuition say that in that institution would give me work, look like a big fancy house such a four- star hotel I am excited in working in the care of Alzheimer's and Dementia, I don't believe.

did not spend a month when they called me to fill documents and start working, I felt very excited, such It seemed like it was my first job, with a good pay.

Well, never before visited any facility until now my idea is take care making the correct work. starting work with enthusiast, quickly know what some Residents don't accepting me; they prefer a Nurse Asist of the same race, instantly realized what I have to deal with that, also with my panics now the important thing I have the job.

I began to identify myself with the residents, helping them in what more could very excited working there.

Not knowing that my way of supporting the residents would cause me big Conflicts with my co - workers. _

just me I knew that she did not do it with the intention of showing that she was the best or taking away he work, in my mind

I just wanted to know what were the ailments of the residents, to see yes my mother also had that disease.

The unwanted day came to my hall one of the residents in the death process, my boss called me for help her and had to go into room but I couldn't then asked another co-worker for help to my supervisor ..

I did not tell them how I felt but I think my companions understood, because they had already the experience and didn't have panic in seeing a dead.

That day was terrible for me, but at the same time my first step to understand a little the process.

a resident on my list dies, she sends me to call my supervisor to help her prepare and put it on waiting list for relatives and funeral home . when she told me to hold his hand to wear her a dress; I knew I had to do it ; but I really don't know how I did it, I felt that for my body passed a sensation too rare that there never was experienced ; but from here were going many situations.

one day another of my residents dies and is ready to wait he funeral car, many times they arrive at midnight, the shift supervisor asked me for some information she need about the deceased to fill out a document, I had to go his room, and just thinking there are a death, walk by the corridors in dim light, any would already imagine how I felt going in the middle of the corridor running, everything quiet and gloomy, only two of us worked in the night shift. _ nor to whom tell him come with me, but I had to do it, I got to the room the light was off I knew that a deceased there so fast as could I turned on the light in the room, the first thing I saw the deceased rigid in his bed. I cannot imagine my fear, the usual prayer came to my mind MY GOD HELP ME, give me strength to do my job, I stayed in the threshold of the door I look at the ceiling it reminded me of the movies when someone dies and ask me will be over there seeing me? I continued standing there watching So inside trying to give me strength to enter until I could do; among the most fast I collected the information and I left running without seeing back until you feel yes could breathe well.

And so Little by little I was overcoming my fear of death "although I doubt it ."

Doing he CNA job, I came up with the memory of several years back when prayed to God, saying : Lord, give me the strength not to have fear of death, since only in thinking that word "DEATH" terrified me, the time was passing and the fear there latent My God has heard my prayer; but it doing difficult for me.

Theme # IX

I DON'T FIND THE EXIT

Many embarrassing situations happened in this facility, I don't know as could bear, such bullying, also they take advantage because my English not good like theirs.

doing the most can I my work, I take care by myself when I doing my work because some coworker check me for the smallest mistake and reported with my coordinator but most the time favored me they did it painfully for bothering me telling thing lies.

Those happened because when I am working in my shift, we all have to do our work very well, and they are looking for a way to get me out there, There were looking for the slightest mistake that I made to report to the coordinator.

Sad when someone resident make me bullying when starting in any activities saying, I don't want the class with you because I not like you accent, those expressions make me feel ashamed, seeing everyone in there, quiet watching me, could react whether to continue or stop, will continue because all activities are in schedule and there no available personal.

but understand the resident, they are sick any in-description is part of his disease my coworker it's just they don't want to see me working here.

I keep doing my job no matter that they could say something bad about me. Always did the best I could helping the resident; I did care wherever if they are or not in my list hall, I did not ignore them.

There were many incredible situations, which were no in my hand. Every day prayer for have a good day. I do that every day, I don't know why; I wonder why I had to endure so much humiliation.

My coworkers make complain even for situation that are no in my hands.

One of the many morning walking down the hall making sure everything in order in the rooms, while the residents in the dining room when close arrive to the door for authorize people I saw a young Hispanic man, coming from other private facility to make a shower to a Resident. from our facility

well he identified with me, both Hispanic he speaking Spanish, well I indicated the Resident's room and we said good bye friendly. What happened the next day in my shift, my supervisor and the coordinator call me for a meeting in the office with both it is for speaking Spanish in the facility, they made me sign a memo and with three memorandum they would fire me.' I STILL KEEP THAT MEMO. FOR MEMORY FOR SPEAK SPANISH.

Successively incidents that did not end, the administration did not fire me, WHY? Will be what I do my work well?

My coordinator knew the person that I am, most of the time she gave appreciation notes and gift card for $ ten dollar for my good work, some co-working still make bullying me. They want put out me from their way?

May I ask by myself why I don't know quit, from this job? Is time to get out?

But I did not, almost going to the true conclusion that my MON did n ot have that disease. I came here for two reason; for a job, then my main changed working there because here it the opportunity what never thinking founding, knowledge about Alzheimer and Dementia. Now I am convinced about my mother's disease. Actually my heart is changing in feeling a special change in my life, can go out from here, I am feeling a special care for each resident, like if they are my family. That disease is so hard.

I started do a lot overtime, every day more and more work, most of my time was spent in the asylum house, when one of my classmates were missing in my shift I be there in the list to work overtime.

I were spending one, two, three six months, one year, two, three, four until arriving To six year; it was cause of conflicts, intrigue when I refused to work for some one.

The coordinator was upset to the point that did not hide his discontent, when I refused to work over time, It is ingratitude since they forgot that I had the right to rest and take care from my family.

I had past almost eighteen months working in that routine seeing alright with them in their rooms. Something happen with me I am seeing them a special affection for everyone, since I know what my Mom doesn't had Alzheimer and Dementia. what happen me? When entering to the facility I forgot that my family existed. Devoting the service to the residents in the facility.

Every day I worked more, and more, tired but it satisfied me, they need attention and more care.

Theme # X

MOMENT WHAT TOUCH ME

In their combative moments. It's a reflect of the Each resident, at times _ combative demonstrated everything that bothered them in their homes, such as fights between family members as with her sisters, husband wife, the death of son and many more situation.

With that disease ALHEIMER, those sad remembrance coming in the combative moment until last days death.

They had mixed feelings before their illness, in their fluent conversations at the Nurse Home, they expressing to her care manager or CNA, or by they self in own room their moments what made them feel bad or happy, reliving those scenes in their combative moment.

I could observe each one and every one genuine with that disease, many They had a great nobility in their moments lucidity, also combative his aggressiveness was more moderate easy mind controllable, but as said all agrees in his_ _ diary live since they _ have use of reason in own home before the illness., I could analyze that each one acted according to his _ living environment. in his lucidity time they had a movie in detail action and names, and the smallest situation that broke their hearts.

All before arrive to the Nurse Home. With that disease relive those tragic moments, becoming aggressive without reason. I was able to observe and analyze that disease develops a behavior according to their livelihoods and their aggressiveness is marked in their education, they have a pattern of behavior.

I was able to differentiate a person with Alzheimer and dementia, in different social class, rich and poor. With or no professional: A Doctor, Lawyer, Military man, or woman A scientist, banker, diplomatic all those professional, and more, that disease comes without any distinction. Their aggressiveness is marked in their education they have a pattern of behavior I was able to differentiate in his combative moment it is incredible but I observed it and lived it. Anyone can say that he has that disease and acts the same to other emphatically no I could say that have his own distinction and control pattern. The aggressiveness all they have; it is moderate, some will easy control.

All with the same disease and aggressive behavior and any one is no comparable to other they have same disease and different form of behavior in his bad and good mode

Remember very well in his agony two residents, in different time and facility. I was able to enter his rooms I ask them how you feeling and simply answered rising their arm tight and with the finger toward the celling; understandable answer. Exactly both answered in the same.

I fell very upset because most the time they death alone requesting for his family. It is sad.

Family doesn't like to hear the harsh question hits them hard. Who are you?

All those observe and learn every behavior for them, since two thousand ten to two thousand sixteen.

When I had two year old working at the facility, I got to the conclusion what my Mom did not have that terrible disease, but I need some more detail to make sure she do not that illness. But I still two more year until I got sick my feet I need surgery, it is when thinking may Asking what happening with my business?. I need back.

With many experience that made me strong.

I return to my business also as Real estate Agent, a little sick, but I sure I'll recover also **very happy because my Mom will not more say what has Alzheimer's,** the very important thing happen me what the facility or Nurse Home was my therapy, because now all my panic was disappeared :

Now I stay alone in a dark room, Now I return off my room light and go sleep, I can see blood in any place and it doesn't scare, I can seeing someone vomit and my stomach doesn't stretch, or tighten, I can feel bad odors and I don't vomit and the most wonderful I can touch a deceased and I not scared and I don't feel those terrible sensations of fear now nothing those scares me, **no afraid of death,** learned that it is a process of another way of living and one day I will go through that process.

Finally Tula **not had ALZHEIMER.**

Which is what has led me to the doubt that my mother does not have that disease?

And that took me many years trying to know if she really suffers from that disease

Theme # XI

NOTHIN EASY IN THE NURSING HOME

Every day those situations make me strong in which I had to get along and fill me with patience. I will detail in chapter some history what made feel sat, few by few it help me to get control to my panic working in the Facility.

SOMETHING UNUSUAL HAPPENED TO ME.

Had about two months working in the Facilitates, one day in our morning break, the _ janitor told me that she not like cleaning the room, number ten, in you hallways,

Because I'm scared in there, I ask her why? I have two nice residents in that room. Asked again why do not like cleaning? and She told me you have not noticed nothing in the room, I told her no; she said did you saw the picture in the side left from the wall the big picture with a big family, Yes I see it every time in the room I like see the big family, always I sit front the picture to observe the big family I told her; I like it She is LDS member they have a big nice family.

The Housekeeping asking again mysteriously did you see anything wrong on the family picture? I said No, it is a normal picture, She said that fine; there are several rows with family in their chairs, but in the last chair at the beginning row, they put the grandson 's chair deceased, and she had a small picture with the decease grandson. Close to the big picture, but the big picture, there is the chair and they say that when they took the picture appeared levitating the body of the young man in the photo, I could not believe, since for two month I was seeing the picture and It look for me normal big family picture.

Since that day every time when going to that room, I looked that picture for many minutes May I ask by myself why I could not discover such as appeared, I looked at it a normal picture. For me it still in surprise, now what can I tell. I have a big surprise in that room.

A morning day at nine O clock, I have to go that room because one those resident need go to bathroom, In waiting for her, I stayed seeing the picture by several minutes, then I felt like rare noise outside I move my face to see the noise outside the window because the noise it's like a fort wind, I looked out and it was nothing, still the resident in the bathroom, I standing still seeing the picture when at the moment could feel someone behind me, and still front the picture but I not turned around my body, but I could see in the same time in front and behind me looked Like a funnel of electricity so fast like a lightning that comes from long way that went through the wall and reached my ear. In that moment it went to my ear I began to feel a pain so deep and strong that felt me fainting.

I fell that someone behind me was touch my shoulder in my main thinking is the resident, so hard to saw around, the pain very strong on my ear, saw the resident in the threshold of the bath door me I ask whom touched my shoulder, what happen here is a spirit? .

The Resident look at me scared, I fell exorbitant because I am filing a lot of pain, sleepwalking I walked some step to grabbed the resident her hand then covered my ear with other hand and walked throw the door quickly, I just crossed the threshold of the room to outside and the pain disappeared, I can believe I felt like I had lived a nightmare, instantly remembered that I had taken a photo with my phone where the Resident young grandson decease and him appear in the big family picture. Immediately look up for that picture and erase. And understood what everything happened to me in that room was because I took a photo that shouldn't have taken and understood that spirits exist.

Theme # XII

INTRIGUE IS A PUNISHMENT

Here came the jealousy of my co-workers, intrigues, restless because I didn't let they do a bad work, they feel that I could write a bad report but that was not my intention, yes known about Alzheimer disease. That why I had to help Residents in the facility.

Their wickedness I will comment on: This incident made me feel sad.

When I describe what made me feel very bad, natural, so upset should to resign but I really don't know why didn't, I can say what there are workers who have no conscience and really shouldn't even remember that incident. My coworker made too dirty action..

"Every day he has lunch with his family"

Every day for lunch was my priority, the first in my list, ready dress in his wheelchair in the meal times, breakfast lunch and dinner, and activities, his family either his _ wife, daughter they came help his lunch, in a conspicuous place in waiting for your family, one of those days we had activities and my classmates had invited to participate That activities day was painting; they use several glasses of water, for the activity, at the end of the activity

I went to bring the residents for lunch, that day I noticed my co-workers very kindly introduced me to participate in the activity that was after breakfast _ I really didn't had idea that it was with bad intentions, however, his friendliness towards me seemed to me good. about that they invited me to the activities, I do not deny that I felt good when they invited me, at the end of the activity were left several glasses of water on the table, I asked the person in charge of the activity if I helped to shoot the water, and she answered no; I will do it don't worry she said, I replied it's fine and I went to get my resident whom were ready for lunch, because family arrive on time to lunch with him.

Well as he is a paraplegic, I requesting for help, his family liked him to be well dressed in his white shirt and black pant, when we done and him ready to lunch that day one of my co-worker helped me put him on in the wheelchair I headed still place safe, visible to the activities manager since she _ helped care for the _ residents than the put in the living room before taking them to the dining room, I left it there in waiting for their relatives, I continued with the rest of my residents on my list were nine So successively until finishing all _ the residents assigned .

when finished left by him to put him in the dinner room soon to -arrive his family, well I approached him and it was so visible that had lying water on his shirt him could saw very wet, I asked What happen with him, in that time no body know. That day I felt so bad, I didn't see it right, I called the supervisor, and no one knew nothing, the administration don't said nothing, I requesting to the Administration in check the Camera. But they say que the camera is private for the administration. But if the family arrived in that moment, will be get a problem with the family, I was very upset close crying, very hard to wearer him in that moment I don't know if will be on time. In that time I need move quit and requesting for help and for dress him.

Quickly asked for help my partner a Hispanic care Manager. Finally I had done before the family arrives.

Since that moment I know that I have to resign that job. I knowing that administration wants not see me there.

Suspected the activities manager since were left the glasses of water on the activity table and she have the responsibility to throw the water. and the resident stay close to where she, also had to be pending of the residents we put ready in the activity room for later _ move them to the dining room .

That day no one knew anything, really me tears came out and nothing to do.

that day God help because, the family from the resident they not look friendly with me, but this resident no body want to take care for him because very complicate he is paraplegic and all easy resident all white care management get. Very hard work they living me

This resident was been a renowned Architect and his _ family esteemed him a lot, therefore they would have sense furious to see the Resident wet; which would be cause to say goodbye me. Cause to resign my work. But when .family arrives there him was no clothes wet.

I asked the activity manager _ you had seen something, she also told me no, at this point all the whites wanted me get out of that place, and the activity was part of the little group that made me bulling, * ** no way the war was there, now it was my turn I need more care with my resident in my hall not allow anything bad toward the residents.

Theme # XIII

NURSING HOME, BOX OF EMOTIONS

Little by little I went overcoming my panic, my fear of blood, of death, the dark, being alone, always I had to be with someone else, my prayers to God strengthened to feel control for wish be really should be common in my life _

Little by little I went seeing situations very different to each person, on my way working in the Nursing homes there were four people who almost acted the same way; reflecting his diary living at first it was uncomfortable; they don't accepting me; I came to think that they were racist and also I thought that with daily deal seeing me_ would change his position; but they did not leave this world with the same behavior aggressive, they very happy with a care manager black or white, not Hispanic many time requesting to the Administration remove me from those Residents that situation very uncomfortably but the Coordinator not removed they still in my list.

I came to the conclusion that it was part of his illnesses. but they no changed his aggressive behavior until death with **Alzheimer and dementia.**

When was working in the asylum or Nursing Home all my efforts were there, the most sentimental when a resident died, sad feeling and our tears in secret,

Their happen many situation very confuise difficult to understand, will be spiritual,things from the beyond when my bodyfilling chills, I think something happen here and quickly leave the place. Fallowing many thing happen will be fanny it depends you imagination and belief.

Theme # XIV

THE FIGHTS WITH DEATH SISTER

There was a resident, who whenever she been in his room.

Could witness his fights with the invincible supposed sister,

I found her talking in voice tall, showed angry, threw objects by all he room such it seemed that someone I was with her, but there was not nobody was; yes his imagination; when I asked her what was wrong? Pointed over said my sister is there, look my room, she has thrown away all my things. Really I found pulling his item all those around the room. I don't know if someone is there, but I not saw any body in his room only she throw all own item found in her way.

observing his performance, start to think and I have the doubt in mind wonder would be so the fights she had with the family?, for some moments I watch to see as enter the room and try to get her out of the drama and back to the reality in a moment we observe all her movements, later with soft words to get her out of the drama saying relax you sister, no longer _ bother you_ we are here to help you, later ended relaxed saying look _ how did She leave my room in complete disorder, we tried to talk to get her out of the drama, it took her hand and we walking outside room.

In he path we talk about things pretty that she liked do in his house, like cook in holidays, with the conversation she forgot the courage with the supposed fight with her sister, when she filling comfortable I left her in the activity room, and she stayed quietly like there was nothing happened.

His sister already was deceased, but she most of the time demonstrating, relive problems relatives. She was of German origin of about eighty seven _ years old. She was very kind with me.

When she passed away, only I met a son who came to her death.

Seeing as his behaved _ in their moments combative; I started to think and doubt arrived would be the fights she had with his family?

Little by little I When known that each residents with Alzheimer 's and dementia, they had a different drama regarding their family, at times of his moment_ combative, that reminded then got in bad mood..

Almost I'm discovering that my mother doesn't have Alzheimer's, but I felt that something else was missing, still had some doubts. Of what my mother has great greatness and wealth?

Now I needed experience to make work by the night, therefore it is where I will give myself account that I have overcome all my fears and the doubt that I have about my mon disease.

Theme # XV

MY FIRST SCARE AT THE FACILITY

Little by little I felt that I was losing the fear and panic to certain situations, as explained before past several months and began to experience situations very rare, I will tell.

There was a resident who was assigned to my care management list, and at night she came to the living room and stay for long time there since she could not sleep, every night when I earing dragging his feet, I said; she coming when there she talking friendly talking about his life.

Her sadness was hanging on his son, because not visit her.

But she not stopped; every day from her room screamed out loud for her son to come visit me. One day the administration contacting him and finally arrive his son and until that day I saw him been in the room; then he left, she stay in the room a little more relaxed, an hour later passed away.

He's came back and left, well I thought the funerary will come by her, but the funerary man, did not arrive, only were appear University personnel since Him donated Her for research on her disease .

Well that's decision is from family resident matter, also nothing to do with the facility.

passed the days maybe about four days of his death, one of those days I had to arrive further early from my night shift, started at TWO IN THE AFTERNOON, that day I was talking with a private assistant

I stopped to say hello, and stood some minutes talking with her, suddenly we heard a loud scream and I ran to the room at that moment I did not realize that there was passed away, I just thought something happening in that room., it was the voice exactly from the resident deceased but at that moment I forgot that she already was deceased., and I ran toward the room, and before entering, the co-work lady with loud voice said, come back that room is empty, she already died, It is until that moment I remembered the resident already was passed away, I returned with the care management and she made me several comments about it with other experience that she had passed in others nursing Homes. Saying are things usually happen, I replied, I will try to get used to it, I went to continue with my work I do not deny a little mortified, melancholic and the panic come back to me, yeah was trying to get over fear of death, but today the panic overwhelms me, we had heard his voice, I do not deny that I think of her miss her visits at Livingroom by night.

Was a lady with lack of affection, lonely?

THE SCREAM AGAIN,

A situation from beyond, May I ask why me? May be She felt something special towards me since me I was paying attention to her conversation, it happened by the night time I did work.

Well, after that, every day in my home, around my bed starting from my husband side bed go around until my side, stayed or no my husband,I heard the Resident dragging his shoes. In the early Morning when my husband go working I requesting him leave the light on then covering my face with the blanket.

One day I had to work overtime at night, from two in the afternoon until nine at night. In the Assisting living building, where the history is complete different from Alzheimer.

that day would be around seven at night we were on the ground floor with two nursing assistants with me, suddenly we heard similar screamed out loud happed in the Alzheimer facility, in this moment we not thinking yes run toward the scream, and another partner said there is no body in that room, go back. But we go check and really no body there, in my main its same screamed in the death lady in the facility of Alzheimer I commandment to my co-worker about the same situation, but they didn't pay attention it often happen, it make remember a co-worker in the Alzheimer facility who told me don't pay attention something hear . or see something not pay attention because you won't be able to work here.

since that day for me It was not good, at my house when was lying down and was not sleep, I listened someone walking dragging feet, I thought is she and covered my face, many time happed it, I had to tell to my husband what was happening to me; since him leaving for work, at FOUR IN THE MORNING, telling him leave the light on, I do not want listen dragging the feet. One of much morning I felt half asleep,

I settled on one side and covering my face when suddenly my dream then I felt that she threw me on the right side of my bed a black bag, I could feel like it was like thirty pounds like meat inside the bag, I felt it there next to my bed, exactly his voice telling me look how they left me. When she told me that, in my main could notice the place and everything she did.

At that moment I sat in bed and I said She is, yeah I understand what she wanted tell me something.

Since his _ son had she donated to the Hospital for research her disease to the medical students. I remember her, cried by his son, an important man who lived in in the City of Park City. His mother deceased was of German origin but very Catholic, and I think she didn't like the ending of her life.

Since that day not more came his name to my mind, either listen to her walk, no more screams, everything went out and I felt peace in my heart.

I had pretty memory when she alive living in the nursing home.

Women and men with that terrible disease at the end of their days died In peace with love to God. Their little faces looked at full of lots peace.

while others with feelings _ difficult to understand, some with a lot Rage screams and kicks, they did not want nor that we let's get closer, difficult see those dramatic scenes. most of them waiting to see there their relatives to say something. but death arrive before. and \ they died waiting for his son, daughter granddaughter wherever, I do not deny that many they died with great nobility, some accepting his death and safe to the path they had sounds.

Two nice Lady in the death process, with that ugly disease, they were very special most of the time with good mood, that day I went in to her room, I stay close her bed, observe for some seconds then asked how filing?, she lifted up his arm pointing the ceiling with his finger, I understood everything, she pointed to the sky, so beautiful; both lady in different facility doing the same, they look pretty lady everyone her face full of peace and love for god.

Sad, family arrives late, they gone.

Theme # XVI

ALL FOR A REASON

After so many conflicts, but I'm still there, One day, my Coordinator told me that I would go work by night shift, difficult for me since the night gave me panic. But I had curiosity if my fears will be disappearing, or may be overcome.

The day came and I had to work by night shift. –Graveyard. It bothered me and I did not feel comfortable. That day was Saturday, well nothing change the same routine like the Morning shift, the most uncomfortable when arrive at nine, at night the lights were dimmed in both hall.

The Night shift only two Nurse Assistant works, we had to attend approximately **THIRTY-FOUR RESIDENTS _in two hall ways_**.

After nine at night _ the residents rest in their rooms, in waiting for their medication, one of as gives the medicine in both, and me make laundry; in that room the washer and dryer and up on the wall long metal furniture, full of hangers, there we hanger the dry clothes

At the back from the laundry rooms our dining room. I stayed watching by select the clothes to wash, when suddenly start in move very majestically the hangers, I do not deny that when I was seeing moving It .I throw it is a normal is no normal, didn't enter air in the room, nothing that could to provoke it movement, never watch it.

The laundry room had a door as in every hospital that closes tightly. I began to feel chills, left it and running, in that moment wanted to fly very scary, and then going with my co-worker., I told her what I had seen.

Very calmly she answered me, said you have to get used to it therefore if not won't be able to here work, his answered made me uncomfortable but thinking she all right. Needless to say, yes looked her, I stayed quiet, don't wanted to separate from my partner, waited she finish her work Then together going to the laundry to finish my work.

The intrigues decreased, my co-worker is Hispanic, she is a funny and hard-working, but I don't know until she accepted me, because of my fears. Well until now I'll see what happens.

In the shift Graveyard I feel better than the morning or afternoon shifts. _

One day the intrigues coming from morning shift, they know what in my night shift I had to finish the laundry.

One those days we had in the night not a pleasant surprise we found a mountain of clothes were even spilling out of the laundry room to the hallway, I went to look the night shift Supervisor and ask her about what happened with lot clothes in the laundry?, impossible we wash those in one day?

Left quickly with my co-work and asked what happened with so many clothes in the laundry room?

She answered me saying the morning supervisor went room by room and take out the clothes to wash.

Therefore no way do not worry, do what you can, will pass several days to finish wash the mountain of clothes.

And without thinking that I would have the proof further strong of my fears, and now I think that everything is given by a reason in the way.

***HERE THE UNEXPECTED.* THE END OF MY PANICS**
"A PAIR OF A SPECTRUM"

I was stand close to the wash machine and observe the mountain of clothes

suddenly I see get in through the door from close the ceiling two ghosts that moved _ _ in the form of birds, they entered together, both moved with the same rhythm, they went straight to the dining room, then turned around the room, going to my direction when they to be in front of me seeing me but hard to describing their physiognomy dress white when they advanced their bodies lengthened like a cloud, or like death persons really longer spectrum, his features hard to describe when I had them in front of me, I fell panic, but I couldn't move, then they continue to the wash machine.

I felt fainting and ran without seeing back felt living a nightmare of my own fear.

That night I didn't return to the laundry.

This day was the end of my Panics. It was the most terrify event then I experimented.

In my mind stay as recorded the spectrums around the room. I don't know as could bear it. Those images was strong will never be erased from my mind, and always wonder, the deceased or ghosts were they looking for their clothes?

That night I did not go back to the laundry; this day was the end of my Panics. It was the most terrify event then I experimented.

Every day I waiting for my co-work to go do the laundry, the mountain of clothes went by almost two weeks to finish.

. Curiosity or courage to know what was happening to my mother, if she has Alzheimer or no. I did experimented many scary situation in the facility, but I am sure what my mom don't have Alzheimer and dementia.

I have much scary history in that facility but I filing satisfy because I learned about that disease and get control of all my panic to the death and many more before I detail.

Theme # XVII

I DID NOT FIND HIM, IN THE ROUND

At the change of shift, out and we enter, when reviewing one of the rooms was scary, for me, the resident was not in his bed.

we were sure they could not escape because all it was locked tight and they would need codes to open the door and escape.

The search was exhaustive, we knew all the space we were easy to visualize the resident all the spaces we were looking for Him, in all the closets, cabinets, doors by bathrooms and everything space that someone could hide.

We were check in the garden possibly heading in there, but was not in the garden. We return to analyze some place where would stay review the house in our main we studied and seen the possibilities He will be in there.

Many ideas in our main, if someone kidnap him. Will be. But need make until the impossible for found him, before call the police.

Suddenness by the yard without leaving an unchecked space before calling the police, we sure that him will be in the facility, ageing we going to the yard would search by the gardens, and we went back to the garden and began to review we starting check all the small dense bushes that were around the house, that day very cold weather and we didn't even fell the frost we were scared, the worst thing was that the shift was ending and they went home. And only two people in try to found him,

we were looking in those bushes without thinking of finding him, since they were very dense and short and the resident very tall 6.6" impossible hide in those shrub, without losing time due do very search quickly and carefully, from last us were left the bushes, and we start from below toward up without leaving no space, and there to the terminal of the shrubbery in a corner was there well in caught, knew what we were looking for him, but neither his breathing we could listen and we had it very close to us, I didn't even imagine it how could _ hide there and the worst thing was that he was alone with his underwear in time cold ; we had lot careful to take him out there.

We began to review him for check him some scratched skin, finally we not founding any scratch.

we feel happy my concern was immense . Nor did I imagine that there would be gone, then finish the inspection we put him in bed and we feel very happy, and avoid the stress in call to the police and family_

It should be mentioned that sometimes in the living experience residents escaped, and found to many blocks near the facility.

In his lucid moment, they want to see family and back home. It is when they try to escape, but the worst in the snowy time. Impossibly to do that it is when they due to depression, loneliness end crying.

Therefor we had to have a lot imagination of ideas to make them return to his environment. That moment is very s

Theme # XVIII

SHE DIDN'T ACCEPT HIS SON LOSS

the residents with the same disease but with a different drama, I have come to the conclusion that in their drama show and act by a situation occurred before his illness, could be from childhood, in the marriage, or by the death of a loved one, especially a child, on all a son minor, is what affected them.

The most People already have this disease coming for their family genes, destined to suffer from Alzheimer's.

One day I arrive a resident with good educated there was obtained a profession accountant, and work in a important and named corporation, I arrive at the facility by warden with very good appearance maybe about 60 years or less, was very kind with good education.

pain more _ big for her was the death of his son in an accident, and could not check their pain, the most times in the morning, she looked at the door from his room, with a worried expression, and when we passed by her door, She said I can't find my car keys, it's time to pick up my son from school, his restlessness was strong, she walked from his door toward inside _ room, and every day she cried uncontrollably left fall to the ground in his fits of sadness he was difficult help her, get over his death son, she remembered him As an elementary school boy, his sadness was strong and passed away in some three months of his arrival at the facility .

"There is no human who does no break their heart in this situation this disease need lot love compassion and patience. They really don't want hurt anyone but there are times when they don't even have control of themselves. That the disease.

"ALZHEIMER DEMENTIA"

Theme # XIX

OFFENDED WIFE

Was a lady that I was observing shown very calm, educated and cooperated for all activities? her husband all the days he visited her for get lunch together, looked older than her, but he look very special with her prepared some food in her house, they looked at each other a beautiful couple, and the most times I was very looking out for them in or more than she could need.

I remember that a night about at nine o'clock we see arrive a resident to the dining room, my coworker and me we were In the activities room that is in front of the dining room, we were observing her, and for the moment she began to beat his hands on the wall very annoyed telling to the husband that she would kill him because he had stolen his house, And many things more, such it looked like as if had face, to face his husband; telling everything she fell for him.

"I got to thinking by what does she say with much grudge. The strange thing that when his husband come and visit her, she looks very obedient, and happy, but to my mind the doubt came, now

I'm learning the disease effects, I Think what there are situation that mortifies her because of his husband ?"

What I can notice in she is that acted such as the husband was in front her, and with the palm of the hand hit on the wall.

I do not deny that it impressed me, my co - worker told me do not mortify what she does is part of her illness.

In his _moments combative many times show a trauma dramatic what the resident had before the disease and express it with courage in his bad mood moment.

Theme # XX

HUSBAND DIES BEFORE WIFE

Had several months since his husband was deceased, after Him death she, was declining little by little, some those day I had to put her in bed, but I noticed that something did not look right in his bedding ; it looked like had several blanket one about another, something told me to check it, while she expected in his wheelchair.

Started to check this bedding and found one of the sheets with poop, the care manager from the previous shift didn't do their job well, it bothered me so proceeded to prepare the bed., she in his wheelchair, talked and talked but I did not put attention to what she said, I needed finish his bed, at the moment calls me and tells me come here there is my sister sitting in soil, I try to see in the place indicate for her but not nobody, I didn't say anything, I just left seeing by some seconds, and more fast I followed making the bed, I felt a little afraid, I wanted leave the room as much as possible fast, when there was almost finished, I felt on the right shoulder gave me two pats on the back, like as someone greeting me back and nobody there at that moment I thought is his husband had patted me; quickly finished and put her in bed, I got out quickly. When I fell in calm, came to my mind that his death husband was giving thanks. But just are ideas that came to my mind.

in the end she passed away months later I was over there in his last days. she was a beautiful lady never bother me she was sweeter lady, was an angel she had Alzheimer, before I said each resident a drama different from each other; with same health condition, high level of education.

Each Resident was an experience to me, and more forgiving control of my fear.

In different situation there were three times what they patted on my shoulder and could feel the difference between a spirit and a human, the spirit is as if someone above me and the tap clap is different.

Theme # XXI

PRESTIGIOUS LAWYER

A professional Lawyer arrived and very religious, I remember when arrive to the facility they only gave him some weeks of life, was _ paraplegic, when I saw him, I said to myself I hope don't assign to me, will be difficult put him in the wheelchair, and all the personal care, but what luck I have good or bad luck?, the same day arrived him, the coordinator assigned to me, any way I don't have any option.

but I remember that the first time I got close to her bed the first thing he said to me very serious asked me where are you from?, I answered him from here; he asked me again where you are from? he knew from my accent very marked Him think what I not telling the truth.

I stayed there without responding in thinking for few minutes and asked myself, I can't believe what if is dying, if is dying why ask where from is the personal to make his personal care.? Since he couldn't even look at me, I told him what also I am a member of his same church, so Could see her behavior change, but not, then I thought he's will be a racist?, since here my work with him so difficult, I had to do it and when couldn't I asked for help.

when I had to do the oral hygiene and tried to remove his dental prosthesis, Him tried to bite me, ageing ask for help and easily doing it my co-work because He couldn't resist him open his mount and made it easily my coworker.

By the Morning other episode train to dress, He, makes his stiff body, and same song asks for help, and easily him tries to cooperate make it easy to my co-work going to dress Him.

When try to transferring from bed to the wheelchair it is impossibly very stiff heavy, ask for help, when my coworker arrive him very cooperate put his right hand over the arm chair, make easy to move on the wheelchair. With me, him very rude, never cooperate doing easy my work.

The worst happen me when his ready dress with the chapel clothes I bring him to the dinner room ready to get his breakfast I try to feeding him, and spits at me and calls me with an ugly word, S of a bitch. Only that word He said to me, possibly malicious that one was remembered. Haw strange he did it without scandal such that he knew what doing. Before I hadn't seen another resident who did the same as him; Well, there are people who grow old and die with certain unpleasant habits, difficult sir, very difficult Sir.

It would be necessary to study if Alzheimer and Dementia has a race preference. But I think yes, I was in other slimily lady.

My life in the Nursing Home was stressful with people like that Prestigious Mr.. and my Coworker showing what the work was easy for them, difficult for me because the Resident made me complicate doing my work with his personal care. Everything was complicate with him until his death, His Family thanked me. But him any his eyes opened to see me, any competition for me. Since the first day to end.. "SAD'

With this Resident learned the work assignments and the most difficult and heavy ones then were assigned to me, also I see the shamelessness of people or co-worker when I look for help, most of them co work show what they doing lot of effort to transferring, because the resident is really heavy, but no; they don't doing any effort; show do that, but not, the maximum effort to transferring was made for me.

I was learning and know that late when I get surgeon on my

right foot and my nerves on the front and down were destroyed the Dr. cut It but still three toes remain immobile. That happened in walking and lifting something heavy.

I remember when that resident I feel heavy to transferring and I saw to easy when my coworker transferring him nothing to say heavy. All those were part of involuntary assignment.

Theme # XXII

CURIOUS ANEUDOTE OF A RESIDENT

"Alzheimer and dementia"

"Similar FIVE STAR HOTE."

One of our many mornings, _ after breakfast time we _ gathered by some moments in expects the _ residents finished his breakfast.

She liked all the good stuff just like to use his own bedding _ _ elegant, everything_ in perfect order, wearing his room like a hotel elegant .

Her body and face were very well care elegant walking, all dress with pastel color with modern style also match with shoes; his conversation was very articulate so that she didn't seem Alzheimer illness, and like she knew where she living.

Really don't remember as it started he topic of conversation, us intrigued the details from her love affairs with **ADOLFO HITHLLER** and that time she had some seventeen years old, and that he always got into at night _ by a remaining door _ in the kitchen of his house.

Each one of us did questions and she answered with very good detail, seemed

to be real, could notice in her features that she enjoyed telling us about their love affairs with Adolfo Hitler.

We wondering _ are true that she was commenting? we are very enthusiast with her conversation, in that moment the care manager supervisor from Germany too said the conversation is done, without comment, simply the conversations are part of Alzheimer's disease, conclusion no more comments, is time to follow working.

I was left with the doubt, since in the previous facilitator of Alzheimer's and Dementia, I remembered a resident, a gentleman Jew with a similar age to Her, this man was in the facility with additional personal nurse, difficult talking with him because the nurse is there, one day He made sure that his nurse was not there, She _ had been located at the entrance of door room, controlling the people who entered the room such looked like rather one _ security service nurse.

Taking advantage of the fact that the nurse was not there close to him, _ seemed to want talk and let us know who was He; began to comment on the way it had been escaped from dying in the gas chambers where Adolf Hitler disappeared to many people, He showed us the mark so that we would believe what he was commenting showing us his arm bliss brand was a series numerical, which did the Germans Nazis to control the _ Jews, who would later those put in the gas chambers.

I remember when this Resident made those comment; immediately came to my mind what had passed to Resident Jew,, difficult, but when he spoke with us he made sure that his nurse was not there, since he _ had a nurse private, which had been located at the entrance of his room, controlling the people my personal conclusion could be that this lady Resident of German origin, could to have state telling the truth of her affairs love.

With the Resident Jew neither doubt

All must stay _ as a simple comment because it was not registered in the facility record. Only the administration should know the true history.

Well Mr. Resident of origin Jew and the German lady, both in different facility, one day after they made their comments, they were removed from the facilities. Who came for them, possibly their relative?

Theme # XXIII

BEHAVIORS SIMILAR TO OTHERS

One day I arrive a Resident coming one of the many ranches from Arizona, when she arrive to the Facility, She looked very good, when they were done questions he knew how to answer them, and easily introduced in activities despite being _ _ _ in a wheelchair it was easy for us despite his overweight.

since arrived this Lady I could appreciate that she is not pleasure look strong towards me, not friendly at me, later assigned to me as always, the further difficult and overweight _ _ they simply assigned. I thought they did because of my personality I am women adult tall and appearance strong, but could _ do no way to do that. Any way that my job.

The first evening when I had to help her with his hygiene care, the first thing he told me do not touch me, I ask her why? She didn't answer, I told her that fine I ask for some help with my other partner, and he did and she was friendly and cooperative.

when we were alone he told me rudeness told me many ugly words, the most times to calm her down and thinking that she would change his attitude, I tried to introduce myself to give her a little more confidence, I identified with her also telling what I am member from the church to which she belonged too, but no, She didn't care for that.

He just said offensive words to me, his attitude was the same, not touch me, and that he leave her as was, The shift that replaced me was a black men nurse 's assistant, she liked to be him, or a white one I explained what was happening, and together we entered the room, she, completely changed his attitude, She was another kind and smiling person, there I stayed watching her and she So Same bad attitude at me, it really makes me feel bad and also could not imagine his attitude, when my co-worker transferred her from the chair to the bed, could see what she did to him easy job, but with me toward force toward down and could feel that I was move a rock it was so visible She look like a racist Lady.

When she in the activities, better If I not appear close at her, because looked at me very ugly.

past several months already I was almost getting used to his way of being with me, and in the end She died without changing his attitude, arrogance towards me, She made me difficult time and worse when had visited by family._

After two year working in that facility they fired me, but bad luck for that because the State comes to supervise that facility.

Theme # XXIV

CONCERNED ABOUT
WORKING IN AN ASYLUM

Really I should have stop working _ in the nursing homes, after they fired me, but there was something that impelled me to continue, perhaps still had question regarding my mother 's Alzheimer 's disease .

Well one day I went apply to another nursing home, makes it easier than really I doubted they would hire me, because people had said it hard go to work in that X institution, since it's nursing home of luxury, for hence already tea can imagine the people arriving there . I don't think they give you a work, without attention to what they told me I was apply since I felt that I have the experience necessary to work there, since Alzheimer's and dementia and would learn more than was learned in the previous job .

Therefore the administration met everything _ the recruitment procedures. Then every week calling to see about my application progress, they always answered me that they were expecting by the record vitae, some reference that there they had to verify.

Wait for a month _ well an unexpected day I received the call to tell me that already they had received all the references that were position in my application and I have to finish with the application, they giving an appointment to make that, when I did that they hired me.

Theme # XXV

ATTACKED ME IN HER BAD MOOD

aggressiveness _ further strong as could experiment, it was with a resident of the colored race, she needed take his shower as every day the employees made complained about her, since she spit on those when tried to help she also tried to attack to my partner work, therefore no one wanted to devise with her and the most easy was assign it to me, they always assigned me the residents further difficult and complicated. No way I had two options accept or resign from the job _ say accept it or leave it I remember when was preparing he water that did not come out very hot, she I unexpectedly caught my hands, twisting my arms, terribly, She had a lot strength, my screams of pain were terrible, I could not reach the alarm to ask help, my cries were strong but it was impossible for them to listen to me since each _ room have secure doors that could not be hear outside unless the door _ were open, There were two doors, the bathroom door and the exit door .

The pain in my arms was excruciating, but the resident had seemed enjoyed it, and wriggled more and more strong, I turned little my body trying that my face in position close to the alarm cord, achieving it reach with my mouth, lucky that my supervisor was very cooperative and arrived running to the alarm call with another co-worker, needed really two people since the resident had a lot strength, she is too aggressive those moments were terrible, it was like a deranged person attacking me, at first she looked peaceful such it seemed that She wanted take a bath, non -opting already the staff had knowledge of his aggressiveness, too before she had tried to attack the coordinator, she attacked me already there was had report of his behavior aggressive .

for me was a experience to get further knowledge about the _ many behaviors associated with the disease, but also could to have had injuries further big if my

Theme # XXVI

AT END THE SAME CONCLUSION

Little by little the I was understanding and realizing that each one had Alzheimer's and dementia, in his life with a different sentimental pain in his life, demonstrating it in their moments combative, dragging up to the disorder of your disease .

in his moments lucid they ask for go home, it is when had to create ideas, like tell them.in mentioned the person who is in charge of them, where they could familiarize. Trying to calm down we talked about dishes, favorite food, something they liked; the most important place where they had fan vacationed or place they like to know starting in mentioned cities like as New York, California and more, if they like some those cities nice because, it's time to talking about until they forgot his bad mood end relaxed and happy ready for the next activity; forgetting the restlessness of returning home.

I do not deny that it made me feeling so sad seeing uncontrollably crying and asking for own family and for go home.

Many they arrived over there deceived, no return. I put myself in their shoes, also in the relatives Why in the _ shoes of the relatives?, because it is to them difficult get along with their relative's illness, they have to work and it is not easy for them since have to be prepared in his time combative so that none out injured, it is the most hard for family.

Many those residents sometimes tries not to be aggressive; some time I saw the effort to get control; whom do that; people with a high education academic his aggressiveness was moderate, and it's amazing those who had some rank military or diplomatic position, or doctors, they tried to control themselves, many sometimes without doing anything _ watching us from a distance

There are times that you cannot believe but yes I realized that yes he resident lived a life without aggression and lived adhered to the code of good behavior, these people in their moments combative are easy to turn into an environment amicably acceptable.***

For me it is the price of life and _ way that I will lead to our final stay for those who achieve get to the hospice, asylum, cannot denying is the final part of our life. Today I realize that I have builds my final stay.

I think that the staff to take care people sick with Alzheimer and Dementia should have special training and patience and so much love for others, I am sure what it's possible to differentiate behavior and control. With patient it is very easily***

Theme # XXVII

A DREAM FAREWELL

The last experience that happened was after I left the hospital, and arrived at my house. After the operation, the anesthesia caused me a bit of a problem. since my body change I could not sleep, neither tried to drink medicine preferred feel the pain a bit and not take pills to soothe it, I wanted improve myself fast .

Three days after my foot surgery, the following happened to me there was a resident who had Parkinson's disease.

Every day she was the last one in going to bed, we talking and I always wondered how I felt about my feet, she knew of my pains ; one of many days do not return to work for my surgeon, well after the operation when I got home, I could hardly sleep had much pain, one night of so many I fell slept, when in my dream I saw her _ I was lying down in my bed, at that moment I saw her in my dream hug me, telling me I have been finally looking for you, she gave me strong and prolonged hug, it was great emotive emotion but followed about me and I felt that I was suffocating, I tried to separate her and I told her you are suffocating me, and I woke up, the next day the supervisor called me to say hello and to find out

about my improvement . Taking advantage of the call I asked for
the resident of the dream and she answered me, she passed away.

My conclusion already was a dream. Tell me good bay.in my
dream she look so happy with me said I looking you.

Theme # XXVIII

MY SAD END AT THE FACILITY

Regarding my panics one of them be alone in a room dark, all the exceed and gladly I will enumerate, now my husband very happy I no longer have to ask him to accompany me anywhere lonely or dark place. I can be alone at home.

panics about death, just thinking in that word terrified me, always begged in my prayers to God supreme in help me to understand and overcome that fear now when I feel spirits around me and hear abnormal noises and smells _ it doesn't bother me anymore . Those no more scare me, my stomach it is already very strong no more vomiting when I look to another person vomit.

Now I can preserve when a familiar dies and visits me, and it's not crazy, almost the same day we give realize that what I sensed was true, I can feel presences abnormal I do not have fear. And only my husband knows what happens to me before, that situation caused me panic I think that everything lived in The Nurse home worth it like as therapy.

In the Facility a learned what the life is short, I'll organize my life choosing what I like for the rest of my life, last option is going to the Facility because the life change there, it is other world no longer decide for wish you like or want, There are policies, code rules many method of discipline." In my option I would arrive there for only a few days in waiting for my death nothing more, I hope it will be.

Now I'm trying to enjoy the moment that I am living in my wonderful days; why say wonderful days? One day I leaf this world and what? I don't need to be a millionaire to enjoin the life yes looking for doing beautiful things that I like and glad the soul.

If you rich in the end you didn't enjoy your money it is sad, or may be better that close to end the life look like more poorer than the poor.

In those ASYLUMS, the days go by so fast with activities in activities until one day unexpectedly no longer get up because death.

Theme # XXIX

GLOSSARY

This small glossary is to help identify specify common name for people and institution that appear in this book but those no showing like as specific own name.

All those with a time to live for specific aged some with specific disease,

Home to live like:

Asylum home, nursing home, facility

Assisting living

Patient: person specific disease or

Old aged.

Resident:

All people living in above institution: Nursing home, assisting living, in some one living for specific aged.

Note

2nd Edition
TULA'S LIES.

All name, place and some institutions, incident are the products of the author; local events, city, or state and people names use in this story those were imaginary and the story is a fiction The story took many years to collecting information until realize that Tula lied about her illness. She, lives in her origin country at own home, with a lot of energy to live with eighty six years old., Peggy still bring money. Tula Love Money. His name will be Tula Money.

All people appear in this history they have passed away. Many those dead for disease covid except Tula she want to alive until arrive to hundred year old.

Printed in the United States
by Baker & Taylor Publisher Services